P9-CND-594

LADY LIVING ALONE

LADY
LIVING ALONE

NORAH LOFTS

DISCARDED FROM THE
PORTVILLE FREE LIBRARY

DOUBLEDAY AND COMPANY, INC.
GARDEN CITY, NEW YORK
1985

Library of Congress Cataloging in Publication Data

Lofts, Norah, 1904–
  Lady living alone.

  I. Title.
PR6023.035L3   1985   823′.912   84-13822

ISBN: 0-385-19475-7

Library of Congress Card Catalog Number

Copyright   1945 by Norah Lofts. First printed in Great Britain 1945 under the pseudonym Peter Curtis. Reprinted in 1982 by Hodder and Stoughton.

All rights Reserved

Printed in the United States of America

PART I

I

In the year 1932 Miss Penelope Shadow published a
book which instantly became a best-seller. It was
her fourth book, and not, in her opinion, markedly
superior to its three predecessors. So in the secret
recesses of her delighted, amazed and muddled mind,
she attributed its success to its attractive title. That
was generous of her, for the title, " Mexican Flower,"
was not of her choosing. The story had left her hands
bearing the prosaic, but exact name, " An Aztec
Tragedy " ; and at first Miss Shadow had opposed the
change and written incoherent, passionately worded
letters in which she tried to make clear the difference
between " Aztec " and " Mexican." But self-confidence
was not one of Miss Shadow's notable characteristics ;
nothing in her past had been calculated to give her
much opinion of herself ; she did not enjoy an argument
or a fight. So before the dispute was many days old
she lost interest, thought, oh well, what does it matter
what they call it ? and proceeded to give her whole
attention to her next book which demanded much
study of the Eighteenth Century Enclosure of Common
Lands, a dull subject which Miss Shadow, by an alchemy
all her own, was going to convert into entertainment.
So " An Aztec Tragedy " came into the world as
" Mexican Flower " and sold in astronomical numbers,
was translated into twelve languages and bought, after
competitive bidding, by a film company. Success, like
a snow-ball, grew as it moved, until the odd little stories

5

whose peculiar flavour had damned them in the days when Miss Shadow would gladly have sold them for five pounds apiece, were to be found in all the glossiest magazines which had paid ten and twenty times that amount for them. And little Miss Shadow, who was slightly stunned by it all, and who had no money sense, except that she hated to be without enough of it, found herself suddenly with enough and more. In fact she was a moderately rich woman.

Miss Shadow herself was one of those women who is never described without the diminutive: a sweet little thing a funny little thing, poor little thing, and, of course, after "Mexican Flower," a clever little thing. Many of the people who thus diminished her were no taller or stouter than she was herself; but there was about her an undeniable smallness, an almost deliberate contraction, a matter more almost of soul than of body. She had the thin light bones of a bird, a low quiet voice, an almost noiseless method of walking, so that always she seemed to take up less room than other people. She had also large grey eyes which were phenomenally long-sighted, so that when she studied any object close at hand—such as the face of a person addressing her, they had to be screwed up slightly in order to focus properly, and this gave her a rather bewildered look which could be quite appealing. But perhaps the feature which was, more than all the others, most responsible for that word *little*, was her hair. It was like a child's, very fine and shiny, pale golden-brown and curling naturally all over her crown in little tapering tendrils.

It puzzled Miss Shadow's women friends that she should never have married. Those of them who were not pretty, and not small, were especially loud in their bewilderment. So small, so pretty, so fluffy, and such a little dear, didn't she just ask for some strong man

to take care of her? Yet, up to the time when
" Mexican Flower " brought success and fame to its
author, who was then thirty-five years old, no man had
shown more than a cursory interest in Miss Shadow.
And it is possible that men, who often show more sense
than women give them credit for in their choice of
life-companions, had looked beyond the little Penelope's
grey eyes, trim figure and lovely tendrilly curls and
seen—or guessed, or in some strange way sensed, that
Miss Shadow was that most uncomfortable, unmatable
creature, a born eccentric.

Moreover, until this last book had brought her money,
Miss Shadow had moved, perforce, in circles where men
look for other qualities than decorativeness in their
wives. And it was quite clear that, be her curls never
so bubbly, a little lady who let her skirt hem trail for
lack of a stitch, and wore stockings laddered from knee
to heel, would take very poor care of a man's wardrobe;
and it was equally obvious that a young woman who
was always an hour early or two hours late for an
engagement, was going to have difficulty over small
matters like breakfast at eight, hot water supplies, and
the weekly laundry list.

And again, however much women may wish to deny
this fact, it *is* a fact that a woman who wishes a man
to marry her must do a little—especially in the initial
stages, towards bringing this desirable state of things
about. After all, Pygmalion, falling in love with a
beautiful and unresponsive statue, is unique enough to
be remarkable; and even those women who most
ardently wished matrimony upon their little friend could
hardly say that Penelope ever " tried." She didn't;
she hadn't; and for the very simple reason that to be
married was never one of Penelope's ambitions. Until
the moment when she heard the breath-stopping news

that " Mexican Flower " had sold fifty thousand copies
before publication, Miss Shadow had cherished only one
ambition, which was to make enough money by plying
her pen—that is her typewriter—to support herself and
help Elsie a little.

Elsie was Miss Shadow's half-sister, ten years her
senior, a widow from the 1914-18 war and the mother
of two children. Elsie received a pension from the
government and eked it out by running a tea-and-coffee
shop in the shadow of Melbury Cathedral. Penelope
was, even before she bought her first typewriter, a woman
of independent means, for her grandfather, who had
not been Elsie's, had left her, his only grandchild, the
life interest upon some property which, upon her death,
would revert to a fund for the benefit of Poor Clergy.
Grandfather Shadow had been Rector of Much Wrenny
for fifty-five years. (Until his death in 1920, Penelope
had lived with him, and although she was hardly aware
of it, a great many of her habits and characteristics
were far more suitable to an aged cleric than to a pretty
young woman.)

Grandfather Shadow's legacy, which had sounded
quite lordly, boiled down in the end to forty pounds a
year, a cheque for ten pounds upon each quarter day ;
and Penelope, vague and unworldly as she was, realized
that she could not live upon this sum unless she could
find a roof under which she could live without paying.
Fortunately Elsie, who had not, for family reasons, seen
her young half-sister for fifteen years, and cherished
rather sentimental memories of a pretty vivacious child,
wrote an eager letter, offering hospitality, and adding,
reasonably, that if Penelope found herself compelled to
work, Melbury offered many opportunities. In any case,
said Elsie, she, being busy with the shop, would welcome
some help with the children.

So Penelope went to Melbury, and, when she remembered the children, was very good with them, fluent with stories, ready with excuses for ill-doing, masochistically ready to sit up at night if one were sick. And if Elsie knew a certain disappointment, if she had hoped to have stockings mended and porridge stirred, or the alphabet drummed in, she never gave a sign. Now and then towards the end of the quarter, Penelope would feel the pinch of penury and would seize one of Melbury's opportunities for earning a living. She had a vast variety of jobs in five years, but none lasted long. She was, despite genuine efforts at self-improvement, the worst employee in the world, unpunctual, untidy, forgetful. Her prettiness—for she was very pretty in her early twenties—might have acted as a palliative to her faults in some cases had she troubled to exploit her charm, but she seemed incapable of doing so. Always, after a short time, she was back home at Elsie's, living through her muddled, timeless days ; not exactly a burden, for there were some jobs she was bound to do, and all but the most piteous fraction of her little income went into the house, but in some sense, as Elsie sometimes reflected, a responsibility, poor little dear.

Then, some time in 1925, at the beginning of the second quarter to be exact, Miss Shadow bought, for the sum of twenty-eight shillings, what everybody believed to be the first typewriter ever assembled. It stood high, with a tower like a battleship, weighed several pounds and when struck—and it had to be struck very hard indeed to shift the worn letters from their rest on the sticky purple pad which inked them—made a noise like a traction engine. With this atrocity and two shillings' worth of typing paper Miss Shadow retired to her room. And for three months she was a dead loss to Elsie who had at least counted on her to answer the house door-bell and keep the fire in. Fortunately by this time both the children were at day school. All day, and often far into the night, the old typewriter rattled and rattled. Incredibly remote, wrapt about, entranced, Penelope would emerge now and then, drink a cup of tea, cut a slice from a loaf, and retire again. Elsie, worried about her health, made suggestions and protests, even, good busy woman, carried up meals on a tray. Penelope hardly noticed, or if she did, snapped that she wanted to be left alone in a manner quite unlike herself. Finally Elsie, with a little shrug, left her to her own devices; and on a lovely June afternoon, three months almost to the day after the purchase of the typewriter, Penelope, blinking like an owl, left the house and drifted to the post office with a big untidy parcel clutched to her chest. Inside it was the manuscript of " The Cavaliers."

A month later Penelope received a letter from the publishers. They had, they said, read the manuscript with interest, and would be pleased to see Miss Shadow as there were a few matters they would like to talk over with her.

Instantly Penelope was seized with panic. She showed Elsie the letter and, after pointing out that they had not refused what she called " the thing," added, " I shan't go. What on earth do they want to see me for ? Can't they write ? "

" Of course you must go," said Elsie eagerly. " But you must tidy yourself up." She made a mental review of Penelope's disgraceful wardrobe and voiced her regretful opinion that there was nothing for it but that she should buy a new suit. " You can have my best hat and . . . yes, my fur. And I can let you have some stockings. A suit and some shoes . . . oh, and gloves. You must, Pen, you must. . . ."

Penelope blinked. "I simply couldn't. I know I couldn't. I should do or say something stupid and mess the whole thing up. Anyhow, what the hell does it matter what I look like? I shall write and say I'm bedridden."

Elsie looked at her with positive hatred for a moment, then set herself to unavailing argument. Penelope did not go to London. Several letters passed, and then one morning came the long envelope containing an indisputable contract which promised to "the author" the sum of twenty pounds advance royalty to be paid on the day of publication.

"What more could you want?" asked Miss Shadow. And by that she meant, not that twenty pounds was the be-all and end-all of her ambition. but that she was justified in her obstinacy over the interview.

"The Cavaliers" had an excellent press and poor sales. Presently Miss Shadow received a further cheque for fifteen pounds and there, so far as that particular book was concerned, profit ended. But, as she pointed out to herself, when at Christmas time that year it was time for her to go to the one regular annual job she had managed to retain, helping the sale of Bumper Books and Greetings Cards at the local stationers, thirty-five pounds was as much as she had ever made by casual labour in one year. So she stayed at home, arguing that there were other people who were in greater need of a light temporary job, and thinking also that it would be rather infra dig. for her to stand selling the Bigga Book For Boys off the shelf where lately three copies of "The Cavaliers" had reposed. And anyway she was much behind with the cardigan which she was knitting for Elsie.

In 1926 her second book, "Roman Holiday," netted her one hundred and seven pounds, in which sum was included the advance royalty for the American rights, and Miss Shadow felt that she was indeed getting on. But the next year recorded a slump and found her actually in debt to her publishers on both sides of the Atlantic. However, Miss Shadow had at last found the job for which she was suited, a job which did not demand regular hours, spurious politeness nor the soul-jarring contact with people ; so, through good years and bad, she persevered with it, having little to spend, always, in theory if not in actual fact, Elsie's debtor, always, if the truth were known a little conscience-stricken because she had chosen the easiest way and always hoping for a miracle, though that hope grew a little less vivid and buoyant as the years slipped away. Then came " Mexican Flower," with sales that were reckoned in thousands, not hundreds, and with all the fascinating accessories of success.

In this memorable year, 1932, Miss Shadow was thirty-five years old and her youth was definitely behind her. The curls of her head were as elastic and plentiful and glossy as ever, but there were silvery streaks in them, hardly perceptible in some lights, very noticeable in others less kind. And that constant screwing of her eyes had resulted in fine lines spraying out from her eyelids to her temples ; and concentration had etched other lines upon her forehead. The determination to live within her means had put nourishing creams and astringent lotions beyond her reach, even if she had been vain enough to desire them, and that same determination, together with the resolution not to eat Elsie out of house and home, had resulted in a further shrinkage of her small body. Appetite, which grows with what it feeds on, had almost deserted Miss Shadow who had nourished it so ill, and she could get along admirably on one meal a day. But, perhaps because at the café tea and coffee could always be had for the asking, she was an ardent consumer of both.

Spiritually, she was still an eccentric, not quite at ease in any world of other people's making ; she was romantic, too—or how should she have flung those nets of enchantment and drawn back people long since dead and shown them living and loving again? And her romantic view was, in part, right. Romance—the belief in the unusual—was justified of her children, for Miss Shadow's own life was romantic in the traditional manner. She had, literally, starved in an attic, she had forsaken the outer world for a world of her own, and now here she was, with money in her pocket and, so they said, a great future before her.

The great future opened, as it was bound to do, with a happy burst of generosity towards Elsie and the children—now big enough to enjoy substantial presents. There was a car, too. And to everyone's surprise and carefully suppressed horror, Miss Shadow herself learned to drive it. That is to say, she mastered the mysteries of making it start, increasing its speed, and bringing it to a standstill ; nervous, inattentive, impulsive and completely lacking in road sense, as in most other kinds, she was quite the worst driver in four counties. But she was not, naturally, satisfied with giving presents and taking her family on outings, and as soon as she was certain about the sale of the film rights, she began to meditate a serious talk with Elsie.

It was typical of Miss Shadow herself, and of the relationship between the two women, that she found this business very difficult to approach. Elsie Cunliffe was a woman of character, and, although for six years she had been extremely kind and more than extremely patient with Penelope, and though Penelope would never have dreamed of allowing her to interfere in anything which really mattered, she was still more than a little afraid of her. To suggest outright—and that was her intention, that Elsie should abandon the shop, throw in her lot with Penelope's, help her in finding a suitable house, and, when it was found, to run it for her, was rather a nerve-quivering process. On the other hand, thought Penelope, bracing herself over a period of days, it was the sensible and obvious thing to do. And presently, when she had marshalled all her arguments, she approached the question from an angle which proved that the people who thought it remarkable that so silly a little creature could ever have written a book were wrong in their estimate of her.

" I've been thinking about the children," she said, one day, casually   Elsie's offspring, Mary, now aged sixteen, and Richard, eleven months younger, were still referred to as " the children " in their absence. " It's a bit cramped for them here in holidays, isn't it ? "

Elsie looked at her half-sister with expectant caution.

" It's cramped for us all," she said.   " It has always been."

" Yes.   And of course I . . ." she did not finish the sentence which was concerned with the idea that her presence had helped towards the cramping. " I've been thinking that it would be nice if we could move ; have a house in the country somewhere, a garden, you know, and a tennis court."

" Yes ? "

" And all live together, of course and . . . well, you could retire and look after . . . I mean it would be easier than this, wouldn't it ? "

" You'd like a house of your own ? "

" That has always been a dream of mine," said

Penelope with a note of apology in her voice. "The country, you know. And I'd like it very much if you and the children. . . . Oh damn it, Elsie, it sounds so pompous. I've lived on you and with you for six years, now it's my turn to do something for you. I want to. Let's start looking about, shall we ? "

Elsie snipped off the thread of her darning, folded together the stockings—they were Penelope's, and laid them in her lap with her hands over them. She looked at her half-sister with affection, and something else, in her glance.

"It's very sweet of you, Pen," she said, "but then you are a sweet person. Look, just tell me this, I don't want to pry into your business or anything of that kind, but have you enough money to buy a house and live in it, enough, I mean, to be able to pay somebody to cook and keep the place clean and look after you properly ? Really enough ? "

"But of course I have. And I haven't finished, Elsie. Now that I'm started I can go on and on. I'm sure of it."

"Well then," said Elsie, "by all means buy a house. But not for us. You see, dear, I have other plans. I'm thinking of getting married again."

Miss Shadow, who had high ideas of feminine pulchritude, and whose heroines were invariably tall and slim and either dazzlingly blonde or smboulderingly brunette, looked with unflattering astonishment at Elsie's square solid figure, high-coloured face and faded reddish hair.

"It's nobody you'd remember," Elsie said hastily. "As a matter of fact he lives in Africa, Uganda. He was here about four years ago and asked me then ; Bob Slade, he hung about a bit but I don't suppose you'd remember. We've written to one another. And now . . . well, you see, it'd be just the place for Richard,

he's crazy on farming and out-door life, and Mary you
know wants to go to Paris next term."

Penelope blinked.

"Then why. . . . I mean what were you waiting for ? "

"For Mary's last term. And to know my own
mind," said Elsie. "But, you see, I had to tell you
now so that you didn't include me, us, in your arrangements, Pen. Though, as I said, it's very sweet of you.
And I should like it if you'd have Mary sometimes in
holidays."

Quite satisfied that her explanation sounded logical,
she calmly took up another pair of stockings and
cautiously inspected them.   But opposite to her Penelope
felt dizzy. It was quite obvious that Elsie had been
wondering what do do about *her*.   She had been waiting,
with God knew what impatience, for some sign that
she, Penelope Shadow, was capable of providing for
herself. Good God, what ignominy ! She had a sudden,
shocking moment of self-revelation, seeing herself as
Elsie had seen her, as Elsie probably, oh, Heaven help
us, had represented her to this Bob Slade who had
hung about, who had been hanging about for four years.
Slothful, incompetent, idiotic, trying to live on forty
pounds a year and eking it out by writing books which
didn't sell. Oh dear, oh dear ! Her never very robust
self-respect wilted and bled. How could she ever make
up to Elsie for these four lost years ? Four years is
such a precious space of time when they lie on the far
side of forty.   And, such is the frailty of human nature,
sandwiched between her remorse and pity was a streak
of hatred for Elsie who had administered this blow to
her pride.

"Elsie," she said in a voice that sounded as though
she were strangling.

"Yes ? " Elsie raised her calm, rather tired eyes.

" You waited because of me, didn't you ? "

" You ? " said Elsie untruthfully, " not at all. Four years ago, when Bob asked me first, the children were too young. I wanted Richard to have *some* schooling and see if this farming craze of his wore out ; and Mary might have turned out less assured and able to be left. As it is, it has all arranged itself perfectly."

But Penelope's quivering conscience was not wholly salved. She felt that she had been a parasite. As indeed she had. For behind Penelope Shadow stretched a long, long line of scribes and daubers, adult in their own peculiar world, but children in this one, vague, feckless, thoughtless creatures always sheltering, consciously or unconsciously, behind some sensible, practical person. But never, never again, as long as she lived, vowed Penelope, would she sponge on anyone, either for shelter or more subtle forms of support. She would even buy another watch, a good watch, guaranteed to go on anybody's wrist, so that in future she should not always be bothering someone to tell her the time or call her to dinner. Oh, she would be a very different woman indeed.

With praiseworthy determination to be independent Penelope set about house-hunting. And of all the pastimes demanding a level head, a practical outlook and a sense of judgment, this is the prime example. Penelope seemed easy to suit, she wanted a house, not too expensive, not too large, not new, in the country, preferably in the Eastern Counties. Her long sojourn in Elsie's top room, up two flights of narrow twisting stairs, had prejudiced her against houses with second storeys ; and that was all. But no sooner had she shown her piquant little face and begun to relate, in her vague rambling manner, what she required, than men in fusty house agencies began to think dark and dangerous thoughts connected with ridding themselves of some "sticker," some house which had been on the books for months, or even years, and had been steadfastly refused by even desperate house-hunters. Penelope, who could be blinded to the implications of a well in the yard by the fact that an apple-tree grew picturesquely over it; and whose thoughts were stirred to vivid realisation of the past by the sight of a roof which was obviously in the last stages of decrepitude, might have fared very badly indeed, and was actually only saved from a sudden disastrous decision by the fact that there were so many apple-trees, so many Tudor chimneys, so many little powdering closets. And while she hesitated, bewildered by the wideness of her choice, Elsie came to the rescue.

Elsie had been vaguely and uncomfortably aware that since that evening when Penelope's house was first mentioned, a barrier had sprung up between her and her half-sister. Twice, when she had been engaged in mending for Penelope, the article in hand had been snatched away and fiercely cobbled together by its owner. Once or twice Elsie's questions or suggestions about the house had been received, not coldly, for Penelope was incapable of adopting a cold manner, but evasively, and Elsie, who was not stupid, had gathered that Penelope wanted to manage the business herself. She could not, of course, guess at the emotional disturbance which lay behind this desire. But she did conclude, with some justice, that unless Penelope had a little help in choosing her house, she would choose badly; and since her own advice was so plainly un-welcome, Elsie, with remarkable kindness, bethought herself of her cousin Babs.

Babs Morrison was Elsie's cousin, not Penelope's; she was also Richard's god-mother; and Elsie's choice of her for that position was not untinged by mercenary consideration; for Babs had married very well and had no children of her own. She lived in Suffolk, in a beautiful old Manor house and was very smart and up-to-date, very thorough and practical. Many people thought she was charming. Elsie, who had often received favours at her hands, thought so too.

She now wrote to Babs, explaining Penelope's position.

"She'll end up with an ' I-beg-your-pardon ' at the end of the garden if someone doesn't take her in hand; and I shall worry about it when I'm gone. So will you look round, and if there's a house for sale anywhere in your vicinity, let me know? Then I'll get her to drive me over to say goodbye to you—though God knows she's the worst driver in the world—and you can bring the matter up casually."

So after all it was, in a way, Elsie who found the Dower House. It was, as Penelope ecstatically said, perfect. It had been built in the middle of the eighteenth century as a home for the superseded ladies of the St. Ominy family; and was now, with the breaking up of the estate, for sale. Probably the St. Ominy ladies, fresh from the space and splendour of Canbury Park, had found it small and cramped; as a house for one maiden lady in the year 1932 it was unnecessarily spacious. But it had all the best features of Georgian building, and, having been part of a wealthy and cherished estate, it had never fallen in disrepair or suffered any of the indignities to which so many houses of the period have been forced to submit. It was built of mellow red brick, had a small, rather formal garden surrounding it, and the front windows looked out over vividly green water meadows which stretched away to Wytham estuary, and the back windows gave upon the thick fastnesses of Canbury Park.

" And that won't be over-built," said Babs Morrison,
proudly pointing out the advantages of her find. " Some
people named Willis have bought it and are going to
build a house on the far side."

" Fancy building a house, when this one is empty,"
said Penelope, with musing scorn.

" It'll be awfully lonely," said Elsie in as diffident
a way as her forthright voice could speak. She was
remembering that over a period of twelve years Penelope's
little foible of not liking to be alone in a house after
dark, had caused her hostess a vast amount of
inconvenience.

Miss Shadow's heart had missed a beat or two as
she too, and for the first time, remembered her abnormal
nervousness.

" It's secluded, certainly, but that would suit Penelope,"
said Babs with confidence. " But I wouldn't say it
was lonely. The Willises will be just across the trees,
there—" she pointed. " And the village is hardly a
mile, even by the road. Look, you can see the church
tower."

Miss Shadow looked, and by virtue of her remarkable
eyesight, could see that the time was a quarter to four.
Surreptitiously she checked it by the new watch on
her wrist, which had stopped for lack of winding, and
even when wound had fallen into the habit usual with
her watches, of losing rather more than twenty minutes
a day.

" I like it," she said, with unusual decision. " I
shall like living here. It's right. And after all, Elsie,
I don't intend to live alone. I shall have servants and
things."

" And after all," said Babs, " I'm only fifteen miles
away, nothing with a car. I'll keep an eye on you."

To Miss Shadow, whose sense of independence was

still raw and smarting, the words had a menacing ring.
There and then she decided, most perversely, that she
would not have Elsie's cousin's eye kept on her. She
had done with all that. She wouldn't have Babs
thinking, or saying, " I must just run over to Canbury,
I promised to keep an eye on Elsie's little cousin, poor
thing." No, if she could possibly avoid it, no one
from now until the end of time should ever spend a
moment or waste a thought upon her welfare. And
as a beginning she would give Babs Morrison to understand that she would be welcome, very welcome, at
the Dower House when she was invited, and at no
other time. Though how in the world, thought Miss
Shadow wildly, such an intimation could be conveyed
without offence, was past her power to imagine. She
shelved the problem for some future consideration.

II

She had taken the house in the year 1932 ; and
Elsie, armed with a luscious and expensive trousseau,
for which Penelope had paid, had gone off to Africa
to marry her Bob, leaving a memory of sudden and
surprising tears, and of jerked-out words of good advice
behind her. Richard in Uganda, which was for him
tantamount to being in Heaven, rode proudly upon a
spectacularly costly mare which was named Penny in
memory of the aunt who had put up the purchase
money ; and Mary had gone off to Paris with her head
full of ideas about fashion designing and several new
trunks well-filled. She had, so far, spent one holiday
at the Dower House, and both she and Aunt Pen were
satisfied with the experiment, and without any desire
to repeat it.

And now, in the first week of January 1935, Miss
Shadow was driving through the premature dusk of a
snow-storm, to all intents and purposes, homeless.

She had said so glibly, on that bright afternoon,
" I shall have servants and things," and had genuinely
imagined in her innocence that it would be easy to
import into the Dower House the prototype of Mrs.
Brazier who had run the Rectory at Much Wrenny
since time immemorial and demanded no help from
either her employer or from Miss Penelope. Penelope,
who had had no dealings with servitors since she had
seen Mrs. Brazier off by train to honourable retirement
after the Rector's death, had one simple theory about
them. You must pay them adequately and treat them
kindly and all would be well.

Thirty months of housekeeping—or more accurately,
of house owning—had scattered these theories ; and,
being the peculiar person that she was, Miss Shadow
had not replaced them by others. She was not
vindictive, she had not bounced off into the opposite
camp which holds that servants should be paid little
and treated roughly ; she was just very puzzled and
unhappy.

She was particularly unhappy on this January afternoon, because, although her car was headed for the
Dower House at Canbury, she knew at the back of
her mind that she dared not cross the threshold alone.
This phobia about being alone in a house had been
the bugbear of her childhood, had extended into
adolescence and now remained, obscenely, Miss Shadow
thought, a fact to darken even her middle years. It
puzzled her. For she knew that in some ways she was
not a coward. She could bear physical pain with
fortitude ; she had once hit, very hard and conclusively,
a lout who was tormenting a cat ; she was not afraid

of burglars, and drunken men held no terrors for her.
But ten minutes alone in a house, especially after
sunset, reduced her to a jittering senseless mass of
terror. Elsie, returning twenty minutes late to the
house at Melbury had found Penelope wandering the
street in a heavy shower of rain, driven out from the
fireside by some vague and unidentified terror. Long
ago Grandfather Shadow had tried reasoning, ridicule,
training, had preached belief in God the Father, had
referred to guardian angels. But to no avail. So
soon as Penelope was alone in the house things happened.
The empty rooms about her stretched wider ; became
menacing with a threat that was the more awful because
it was unnameable ; became unendurable. There were
noises, too, faint tickings and shufflings, easily explained
by other people as due to the expanding and creaking
of old timbers. And yet Miss Shadow was not really
afraid of ghosts ; but she was afraid of the dark and
inexplicable change which came over familiar places as
soon as she was alone in them. Outdoors, for some
reason, held fewer terrors, and on this cold cheerless
afternoon she was determined, at the beginning of her
journey, that if the worst came to the worst she would
spend the night in the car in the lane that ran before
her house.

The predicament in which she found herself was
partly of her own making ; but only partly. Ten days
earlier she had left the Dower House in charge of her
current housekeeper and general factotum, Miss Dewhurst. Penelope was going to spend Christmas with
the one friend which her profession had made for her,
the celebrated Miss Caroline Fletcher ; and Miss Dewhurst
was going to act as hostess to her sister and brother,
a doddering, pathetic couple of distressed gentlefolk.
It was an admirable arrangement ; and Penelope,

before leaving home, had spent two or three very happy
days bringing Christmas food and little presents and
every comfort and luxury she could think of from the
local town, Strebworth. She had even, she who had
never dared ask the daily woman, Mrs. Paine, for a
favour in all the thirty months she had employed her,
given definite orders that fires were to be lighted in
both bedrooms every evening and renewed again in
the morning ; and she had driven away feeling warm
and comfortable herself because she could imagine how
very warm and comfortable the poor old things would
find the Dower House after their poverty-stricken
cottage.

All through her stay with Caroline Fletcher she had
been aware, at the back of her mind, of the three
Dewhursts basking in her house. But on the second
of January she had received a letter from Miss Dewhurst,
who was very much the youngest and most able-bodied
of the three, which had shown her how wrong the
best-laid plans can go. It was a long, extremely
involved letter, written up and down and round about
the pages after the fashion of a generation bygone ;
but the gist of it was that Miss Dewhurst had slightly
misrepresented to her family the conditions under
which she laboured ; they were shocked and horrified
to discover that apart from the daily woman she was
the only help Miss Shadow employed. They did not
like the idea that she actually did the cooking. They
were appalled by the fact that she had to make the
early morning tea. In short, they had insisted that
when they left the Dower House she should return
with them to their cottage, to have a good rest before
looking for another post, where, they must insist, a
resident maid would be kept. Miss Dewhurst was very
sorry if she was about to cause Miss Shadow any in-

convenience; but as Miss Shadow knew, her health
was very delicate and both her brother and sister were
mainly considering this in urging that she should fall
in with their plan, which was that when they left
Canbury on Saturday, they should take Miss Dewhurst
back to the cottage where she could have a good rest
before seeking another post. Miss Dewhurst was certain
that Miss Shadow would understand.

Penelope, screwing her eyes over the barely legible
screed, understood perfectly. Understood that, between
ladies, one of them in delicate health, rude matters
like a month's notice must never be considered. She
understood, too, for she could build up a whole situation
from the slightest clue, just how far the elder Dewhursts
had been deceived; and just what part discontent and
resentment at being the one to have to earn a living
had played in Miss Dewhurst's decision. She cursed as
she tore up the letter and the full-flavoured, nautical
oaths which she had culled from her historical researches
and used partly to keep them in mind and partly
because they appealed to her, sounded odd upon her lips.

She did not mention Miss Dewhurst's defection to
Caroline, who, although she did not know about
Penelope's fear of loneliness, would have seen the
practical disadvantages of a return, in mid-winter, to
an empty house. Caroline would have extended her
invitation, pressingly and indefinitely; and that would
mean that Caroline, like Elsie, would be putting herself
to inconvenience for the sake of poor little Pen. So
Miss Shadow had driven away on the day and at the
time previously arranged, deriving wry amusement from
Caroline's query as to whether she had made certain
that a hot meal would await her at the end of the long
cold drive.

And now, mid-way between Storford and Strebworth,

she was driving into a snow-storm ; she was afraid to go
home ; and she could think of no alternative destination.

Dejectedly she set her windscreen wiper in motion
and to its measured ticking pondered her domestic
problems. She simply for the life of her could not
see why, in thirty months, she had changed housekeepers five times. The morning room of the Dower
House had been pleasantly furnished as a sitting-room ;
the bedroom above it held every amenity which was
to be found in Penelope's own. Mrs. Paine, a vast
genial widow from the village, came across the fields
every morning at seven o'clock and began her good-
natured round of not-very-efficient cleaning and continued to pursue it, with intervals for refreshment, until
five o'clock in the afternoon. And though she didn't
sweep in corners or dust ledges, or worry unduly about
crevices and crannies out of easy reach, neither did
Penelope, and the woman's mere presence absolved the
occupant of the housekeeper's room from the bugbear
known as "rough work." What then remained ?
Penelope asked herself ; what was the mystery ? in
what way had she imposed upon Miss Dewhurst's
delicate health ? The housekeeper planned the meals
and did the shopping. Several tradesmen called with
vans in the course of the week ; there was a shop of a
kind in the village, the bus to Strebworth ran past the
end of the lane on certain days, and if these defences
failed there was always Penelope, meekly (and to any
other eye, foolishly) ready to leave her work and go
into town to buy a packet of gravy salt. She never
questioned a bill ; she had paid each successive bully
two pounds a week, a sum which had made Babs Morrison
scream when she was told in answer to her cautious
question, "Do you pay them enough ? " upon the
occasion of the third housekeeper's going. And, reflected

Miss Shadow, remembering the time when Miss Slater, a vegetarian, ruled the house, I'm very obliging. For she had said, hadn't she, "It seems silly to bother with meat for one, Miss Slater, I'll eat just what you do." Highly peculiar things they were, too, she thought, brooding upon the memory of nut sirloin, and palm oil stew.

No, it couldn't be the fault of her parsimony, or her intransigence that this thing had fallen upon her. She had even brought intelligence to bear upon the subject; she had tried different kinds of women. Mrs. Grant had been a bit of a mystery, her husband was never really accounted for; she was a good type of working-class woman who had run a working-man's lodging house until a rival establishment ruined her trade. She had been Penelope's first housekeeper and had settled down with expressions of happiness. At her hands her employer had suffered, without complaint, a surfeit of steamed puddings, hot-pots and hashes of the kind which had doubtless, in former days, gladdened the palates of many sturdy men hungry from manual labour. But Mrs. Grant missed the company to which she had been accustomed, and she had followed Penelope about, especially in the evenings, regaling her with long, involved, pointless stories about "the men," all told in a flat, excrecable Essex voice. And although Penelope had borne that with fortitude, only putting up the piteous defence of tapping the shift bar of her typewriter in intervals of thought lest the silence should bring Mrs. Grant in for a chat, Mrs. Grant had left at the end of three months pleading that she found Canbury too lonely and that she must seek a post where there were more people. It was a legitimate excuse and Penelope never even examined it critically. But she did choose her next house companion, Miss Slater, on account of her voice, which was low and agreeable.

Miss Slater was a poor thing, a bad case of ingrowing virginity; pallid, ailing, a rabid vegetarian, a student of Theosophy, Yogi, and Re-incarnation. During her brief stay at the Dower House Penelope enjoyed for the first time the experience of being the strong spirit in the house; she had mothered Miss Slater and spent a good deal of time devising ways of circumventing the rigid rules of her diet. There was, she discovered, a preparation called Concentrated Beef Juice which could be popped at the last minute into vegetable soup and remain undetected. Penelope would send Miss Slater out of the kitchen for a moment when the pots were bubbling unsavourily upon the stove and empty a bottle of the valuable preparation into the first saucepan which came to hand. Miss Slater's breakdown at the end of four months was quite genuine. She attributed it to uncongenial auras, whatever they might be; and the adjective at least may have referred to Mrs. Paine's staunch loyalty to her carnivorous beliefs; there had been trouble when Mrs. Paine, after Penelope's feeble adoption of the vegetarian rule, had brought her own lunch, thick slabby sandwiches of roast beef.

" No, no," she had said in reply to Penelope's protest that food was included in her contract, " I don't mind bringing my own bite. But face that cat-lap again I jest can't." Her remarks upon the subject of " cat-lap," when addressed to Miss Slater, were more pungent and less tolerant. Anyway, Miss Slater collapsed on a cold spring day after an orgy of raw grated cabbage sprinkled with pea-nut dust, and when Penelope, desperate, earnest and fumble-fisted, had sent for the doctor and nursed her back to some semblance of health, she had gone off to join what she called The Group, some mysterious place where, presumably, all the auras would be congenial.

Mrs. Meadows, her successor, was frankly dishonest;

but it had taken Penelope almost a year to discover the fact and a further two months before she could bring herself to mention the matter. Perversely enough, Mrs. Meadows had been the most efficient and the most congenial occupant of the post ; and after the scene which had resulted from Penelope's rabbit-nervous questions about bills sent in for the second time, she was spinelessly sorry that she hadn't paid them again, and again after that, if necessary. Mrs. Meadows had departed in a flurry of hurt feelings, and loud protests of integrity, having saved the whole of her salary and netted some sixty pounds besides.

Penelope's fourth attempt brought her a born incompetent, dirty and truculent, whom even she took pleasure in dismissing. Then had come Miss Dewhurst, a lady, possessed of enthusiastic references from distinguished people, tactful, self-effacing, not much of a cook, but well able to deal with Penelope's simple needs. And if Penelope hadn't, in kindness of heart and simplicity, planned a treat for the elder members of the family, Miss Dewhurst would be there now, with a fire and a meal of a sort and some hot water, with, above all, the blessed assurance that there was another human presence in the house, enough to keep those other inhuman presences at bay, to stop pictures leering suddenly and fixtures from shifting stealthily about.

Just as Miss Shadow's thoughts had come full circle and reached the dispiriting point from which they had started, the car skidded, seemed to travel several yards along the road broadside on, and then came to rest with its nose against a mound of sugar beets, piled near a gateway to await transport. Only then, looking round at the rough tussocky grass filmed over with snow, and at the half-obliterated surface of the road, did Miss Shadow realise the conditions through which

she had been driving so thoughtlessly. And as she did
so a little thought of comfort budded in her mind.
Even normal people who were not afraid of their own
houses, even fortunate people who had not lost their
housekeepers, might be waylaid by a snow-storm. It
was the kind of thing which might happen to anyone.
And the thing to do was to drive on carefully, attending
to the business, especially at corners, and to keep a
sharp look-out for a place in which to stay. Then she
could telephone to that kind Miss Shrewsbury at the
Registry Office and it might be possible that a new
housekeeper could be installed immediately, tomorrow
even. Once before Miss Shrewsbury had " fitted her up,"
as she called it, within twenty-four hours.

Impatience ran like a fiery tremulous liquid through
Miss Shadow's bones, pressing her foot down upon the
accelerator, making her hands unsteady on the wheel ;
so that at the foot of Hawberry Hill she had another
skid, milder yet somehow more frightening than the
first. After that she slowed down against her will and
so came purring into Hawberry itself. She was keeping
what she considered a sharp look-out for a likely hostelry,
but her vague, long-sighted stare, busy with observing
every detail of the horrors of the "Four Pigeons"
which announced itself as offering good pull-in and
beds for lorries at the far end of the street, missed
entirely the red-curtained comfort of the "Unicorn"
which she was just passing ; and the little town, with
its one street, slid away and was behind her, leaving,
so far as she could remember, nothing but a pretty
desolate stretch of road between her and Strebworth.
And she wanted a place nearer than that, she wanted
to telephone immediately ; and she wanted to be
weather-bound in a place really out of reach of Canbury.

Afterwards, through vastly varying moods, her fancy

would play with the idea that Fate had been with her
on that afternoon, guiding her actions, moulding her
very thoughts. And, oddly enough, though everything
within sight was by this time thickly coated with snow
which was falling so fast that Miss Shadow had twice
had to clear the accumulation of it from her windscreen
where the wiper was clogging, the momentuous notice-
board, with its back to the wind, was clear and perfectly
legible. From a great way off Miss Shadow read its
exhortation. " Turn Left," it said, " for the Plantation
Guest House. Historic Surroundings with Modern
Comforts. Golf. Riding. Fishing. H. and C. in all
rooms. Terms Moderate."

Made for me, said Miss Shadow aloud. She had
contracted the habit of talking to herself when alone.

At the next left-hand turn she swung the car and
seemed to enter immediately into peace ; for a thick
plantation of larches and fir trees now stood between
her and the north-east wind. The rough gravelly
surface of the secondary road seemed only lightly
freckled with snow. Miss Shadow's foot came down
again and she almost speeded past the Plantation Guest
House which stood back from the road and only announced
itself by a board over its dignified front door. Miss
Shadow braked hurriedly and, being too near the first
gateway to turn easily, crawled on a few yards and
entered by the second one. Between the house and
the road lay a stretch of lawn dotted with small iron
tables, each with a hole in its centre for the reception
of the support of a gaily coloured umbrella—surely,
thought Miss Shadow, the most dismal sight upon a
snowy January afternoon. In summer—and yet something told her that it was not last summer but in
summers farther removed in time—the Plantation Guest
House must have been a pleasant place. Now, with

its Palladian grey stone front, just the colour of the
sky above it, its background of almost black fir trees
and its blustering drift of greasy-looking yellow smoke
rising from a square chimney stack, there was something
sad about it.

Penelope stood on the step and pulled the iron handle
of the bell Far away she could hear the resultant
clanging But no one came in answer and, stepping
back, after the inconsequent fashion of neglected bell-
pullers, she took in a view of the house front It was
Georgian, and far grander than her own, and since its
history was unknown, seemed less the abode of peaceful
retirement than the Dower House must, by virtue of
its very name, have been One could imagine life
being lived ruthlessly here, weaving a tapestry of
grandeur and hauteur, and jealousy and passion. Even
as she smiled at her fancies, remembering Miss Slater
and her babble about auras, Penelope's mind slipped
away into the world of periwigs and gallantry and wax
candles above stairs, of chilblains and overwork and
rushdips below. For one of the reasons why Miss
Shadow had had to wait so long for recognition of her
talents was that she was never dazzled by red heels,
and lace ruffles. While her right hand tapped out its
web of entrancement her left added little rough nuggets of
realism, and each hand knew what the other was about.

It was perhaps five minutes before she rang the bell
again, for her far-seeing eyes had spotted, to the left
of the house, at the end of a long garden, a little white-
pillared summer-house. It spoke of trysts on summer
nights when skirts would be held lest the stiff silk rustle
betrayingly on the dewy grass. Oh rich and colourful
past ! What enchantment could distance in time supply!
Almost dreamily she pulled the bell again, and then,
with one of her sudden disconcerting impulses to self-

assertion, a third time, before the bell had ceased
jangling from the second pull. Now the door opened
abruptly and within the dark shadow of its hinterland
stood the person of whom Miss Shadow was for some
time to think as The Boy.

He would have seemed, even to an eye less perceptive,
less colour-lustful than Miss Shadow's, a very beautiful
boy. One was immediately conscious of bright blue
eyes, the brighter for being narrow, as though tightly
bound by the black-lashed lids. And his hair was
arresting, too, being a deep red-brown, just the colour
and glossiness of a horse-chestnut, autumn freed from
its green husk, or of the polished deep-upon-deep of
mahogany wood, or of certain brown sherries. In shape
his face was square, with a jaw which time would thicken
and spoil but which was at the moment just pleasantly
firm ; his nose was short and blunt, slightly snubbed
at the very tip, and his mouth, rather large and thin-
lipped, quirked at one corner.

Miss Shadow, though she could safely and blamelessly
say that she had never drawn a character from life, was
perpetually on the alert for striking physical features,
little tricks of movement, turns of speech. She noticed
them and promptly forgot them—had in fact, during
the Melbury days, often given offence by passing with
unrecognising eyes, people to whom Elsie had introduced
her. But later on, when Miss Shadow moved into the
world where she was competent and wide-awake, she
would find awaiting her, all beautifully preserved, the
fruits of her observation.

So now, half consciously approving, half unconsciously
storing away, she stared at the boy's face, and then
let her eyes drift over his body, which was so thin that
he looked taller than he was, and which was girt round
the waist by an apron of a surpassing filthiness. The

sleeves of his poor blue cotton shirt were rolled up
above his elbows, and his forearms, though corded with
muscles and heavily haired, were slightly pathetic in
their immaturity.

" Were you wanting to stay here ? " he asked.   His
voice was pleasing, lilting, unmarred by any accent.
Irish, thought Miss Shadow, pleased with her perception.

" Yes," she said.   And although he had torn open
the door widely, as though impatient, and it now stood
as wide as it would go, he made, by giving it a fruit-
less tug, and stepping backwards, a gesture of welcome.
As he did so Miss Shadow saw, below the apron's edge,
the ends of black trousers, spattered with grease and
a pair of broken patent-leather shoes.

" I'll call one of them," he said.   Then Miss Shadow
saw his eyes focus, with an expression of avidity, upon
something behind her back.   " Would you like me to
put your car away for you ? "   It was more a request
than an offer ; it said may I ?   Do let me !

How young, thought Miss Shadow, remembering how
Richard had teased her into breaking the law by letting
him drive in lonely places.

" Why, yes," she said.   " Certainly, that is if I'm
able to stay."

" Oh, you can stay," he said.   And the assurance
of his manner convinced her that he must be the son
of the house.   He plunged into the dimness that lay
at the back of the hall, behind the spiralling staircase
and called in a different, distinctly less amiable voice,
" Miss Beasley !   Miss Beasley ! "

He disappeared, still calling, and several moments
passed.   Miss Shadow occupied them in staring about
the hall.   Empty it would have been lovely with its
elegant proportions and creamy panelling ; but its

furnishings were hideous ; the carpet looked as though
pounds of liquorice all-sorts had been stamped viciously
into mud ; there was a fiercely bristling hatstand, a
Windsor armchair painted a bright sticky red, and the
panels were defiled by pairs of Victorian pictures, hung
irregularly ; Beckworth Bridge in summer and in
winter ; lovers parted and re-united, married couples
quarrelling and making it up again.

As she looked, disliking everything she saw, she
became aware by that peculiar sense which seems to
be a legacy of primæval days, that someone was watching
her. Swinging around she saw, for a brief moment
before it was hastily withdrawn, the face of a woman
who was peering out from behind a half open door.
It was a mad white face with a scarlet slash for a mouth
and two dark hollows for eyes. A little shudder of
repulsion rang down Miss Shadow's spine. She was
convinced that this was a horrible place and her longing
for comfort weakened into self-pity. Oh why couldn't
she be on her way to her own home ? Or, failing that,
why couldn't she have found some cheerful, comfortable
lodging. Or again, compelled to be here, why couldn't
she win some attention and not be left standing in this
cold, ugly hall ?

As though in answer to her third question, the boy
came darting back out of the shadows. A rug skidded
under his feet and he swore softly ; but, passing Miss
Shadow on his way to the front door he said genially,
" Sorry to keep you waiting. She's out, but I'll find her."

He had left open a door somewhere back in the
shadow and a new, more aggressive draught allied itself
to those already astray in the place. And presently
four large mangy cats strolled in, looked at Miss Shadow
superciliously and proceeded to play some lively and
complicated game on the stairs. Miss Shadow, who did

not care for cats watched them for a moment with the fascination of repulsion.

Then she heard the boy's voice, recognisable, though speaking indistinguishable words, outside the front door. A woman's shrill and irritated said, " Don't argue with me. Don't *argue.* Go and get on with your work."

The door opened and the owner of the female voice stepped briskly within. She was small and plump and completely Edwardian. Under her grey woollen dress her figure was so corseted that her bust and hips looked hard. Her iron grey hair was dressed in a high hard pompadour ; her throat was encased in a high lace collar, held stiff by supports ; gold pinc-nez hung on a gold chain from her bosom on one side, balanced on the other by a gold watch pinned with a true-lover's knot with a turquoise in its centre. Miss Shadow knew, beyond the possibility of doubt, that Miss Beasley had been a schoolmistress. As she entered the door she swung from her shoulders a mackintosh cape, adding it carelessly to the huddle of similar garments on the angry hall-stand.

" I'm sorry you have been kept waiting," she said in a prim cool voice. " The boy knew where to find me. I told him. But he never listens. You were wanting to stay ? "

Miss Shadow nodded, neglecting to speak because she was engaged in the endeavour to see why this Miss Beasley, with her firm, high-coloured face, her tight pale mouth and her rather prominent eyes should appear at first sight so definitely, so undeniably related to the woman with the mad white face which had stared around the door. There really was no reason ; two faces, both English, both female and both past middle-age could hardly be more dissimilar, yet Miss Shadow knew that the women were sisters, just as she knew that

the woman who was now asking, " For how long ? "
had been a schoolmistress. Just one of my leaps in
the dark, thought Miss Shadow, bringing her thoughts
back to frame an answer.

" I'm not quite sure. At any rate until the weather
is better. It depends. . . ."

" I see. Well, I can show you a room and the boy
can bring up your bags. Come with me."

She stepped ahead of Penelope into the seething mass
of cats on the stairs. " Dear Malkin," she said, patting
a long stiffly uplifted tail. " Do you like cats ? "

" Not much," said Penelope, edging past.

" Such a pity, I always think," said Miss Beasley
coldly. " Still, I suppose it can't be helped. Lord
Roberts you know."

The title, spoken in that tone of voice seemed to
pronounce absolution for an error of taste. Yes, thought
Penelope, I know. And in a thousand years, when his
campaigns are one with those of the Hannibal, that foible
will ensure his immortality.

" Now I always think this is a very pleasant room,"
said Miss Beasley, daring anyone to think otherwise.
It was, like every other room in the house, a pleasant
room, but it was execrably furnished, and it struck
a further chill even into Penelope's freezing frame.
A big high bed stood in the middle of the room, looking
lumpy and inhospitable under its cold white-honeycomb
quilt.

" Is the bed aired ? " she asked, putting the question
in a loud voice because she had to overcome a reluctance
to ask at all.

" All our beds are aired," said Miss Beasley positively.
" And there's a gas-stove. It works from a slot, a
shilling. Well ? "

" Oh yes. Thank you. It's very nice," said Penelope,

sacrificing truth to the weak desire to make Miss Beasley
look at her less disapprovingly. " Perhaps I could have
a . . . a hot bottle in the bed. I have a tendency to
rheumatism," she explained, " that's why I'm so fussy."

" You've no call to be, here. However, of course,
you may have a bottle. I'll tell the boy about it when
he brings up your bags."

" Oh, I have one of my own," said Penelope eagerly,
trying to forestall the idea that she might be giving
trouble.

Miss Beasley received the remark in silence. Penelope,
looking at that firm hard figure, that red, slightly
roughened complexion, could imagine her plunging into
a cold bath each morning and into an almost equally
cold bed each night, one of the old school, no pampering.
Did that augur well of the food ?

As though she had read the thought, Miss Beasley,
on her way to the door turned and asked, " Are you
fussy about food ? " (As you are about beds, was the
unspoken addition.)

" Not a bit," said Penelope with complete truth.

" Can you eat beef ? "

" Oh yes."

" Well, it's mutton tonight. Dinner is at seven."

No mention of tea, thought Penelope mournfully.
Then the peculiarity of the question about beef and
the statement about mutton, put in that order, struck
her. And she remembered the mad face and its incredible
likeness to the sane one. Probably this Miss Beasley
was a little mad too, only able to keep it in hand,
leashed, as it were, and only snapping out now and
again as in those words about beef and mutton.

She walked to the gas stove, a hideous brown
enamelled thing with several gaps in the asbestos. She
found a shilling and her cigarette lighter—Elsie's parting

present—turned the tap and applied the flame. A pale
discouraged glow crept for about three inches along
the bottom of the stove ; and a noise like a train going
through a tunnel filled the room.

Penelope lighted a cigarette and kneeling down held
her little cold hands to the credited source of heat.
Very little came out to meet her. I'm cold and I'm
hungry and I seem to be a prisoner till seven, she
thought ; and knew that she herself should have
mentioned her need of tea ; and asked the terms too.
Imagine Elsie, or Babs, or Caroline allowing themselves
to be poked away here. Even Mary would have
managed better.

She was half-way through her cigarette which meant
that it was about five minutes since she had lighted
the fire, when with a final despairing scream it relapsed
into inactivity. Impossible, thought Penelope. Twelve
shillings an hour, seven pounds odd for a twelve-hour
day, nearly fifty pounds a week. What are your
overheads, Miss Beasley ? Well, my fuel comes rather
expensive. At this rate what would it cost to cook a
joint of meat, beef *or* mutton ? Still, she would freeze
without the poor illusion of warmth which the stove
supplied, so she raised herself to seek another shilling,
and, pulling herself up by the mantelshelf, felt a coin
under her fingers. She had found it, but she had not
put it in the slot. And you are the one who thinks
other people look mad and sound mad, she thought,
stooping to find the slot. The coin stuck in it, neither
in nor out, stubbornly refusing to be pushed further or
to be withdrawn.

Tears of exasperation welled up in Penelope's grey
eyes. It was all so dreary, this enforced exile, this
awful weather, this queer house, that very suspicious-
looking bed, and now the stove. A knock sounded on

the door. Penelope blinked to disperse her tears before
calling " Come in " and merely succeeded in squeezing
them out on to her cheeks. She plied her handkerchief
swiftly. The boy opened the door and carried in,
lightly as though they were feathers, Penelope's heavy
cowhide suitcase, her matching, well-named " hold-all,"
and her portable typewriter. He had donned a seedy
grey jacket and a rough woollen scarf and upon these
as upon his hair lay clear drops from melted snowflakes.
He glanced at Penelope and then hastily averted his eyes.

" I put her away," he said.

" And I've jammed the stove," replied Penelope.
She was very small, very pathetic, just then, diminished
and undermined by cold and despair.

The boy bent over the stove, straightened himself
and drew a knife from his pocket. There was a
scratching sound and then the re-assuring drop of the coin.

" Have you a match ? " he asked, and stretched out
his hand without turning his head in her direction.
Penelope flicked the lighter and put it between his fingers.
The stove gave a great plop and roared eagerly.

" Now," he said, turning, but still not looking at her
face, " you're wanting a bottle, aren't you ? "

" Oh yes," said Penelope. She went over to the
suitcase, laid it on its side and pulled back the catches.
One flew up, obligingly, the other stuck. She wrestled
with it fiercely, hurting her thumb, knowing that it
was not locked for the key had been lost, un-used,
within a fortnight of the case's purchase. The boy,
with an air of humorous patience said, " Let me try,"
and moved towards her. Unwillingly she stepped aside,
and he pressed the catch which clicked back, and the
overstrained lid of the case flew up and the full horror
of Penelope's packing lay exposed to the eye of a strange
young man. Jumbled together, as haphazardly mixed

and as inextricably entwined as were the conflicting
elements in their packer's nature, lay the black chiffon
nightdress which she had bought in an extravagant
moment, the thick knitted bed-jacket with long sleeves
which she must wear over it because she felt the cold,
and slept alone and had a tendency to rheumatism,
some solid silver toilet articles which announced that
she could now indulge her taste for good quality, and
the slippers with the mended soles which could not be
thrown away because the uppers were still good and
Penelope had learned the lesson of penury, a bottle
of sleeping tablets, a packet of digestive powder, the
edge of a thick wad of typescript, a box of cigarettes,
a packet of salted almonds, a silver brandy flask with
a screw top which was not quite watertight, and four
very dirty handkerchiefs stained with nicotine and
lipstick. It's a slut's baggage, thought Penelope, as
she gazed over the boy's arm, and saw the confusion
and smelt the mingled scents of escaping brandy and
stale " Sandalwood," a flask of which had been a
present from Caroline and therefore used profusely
throughout the week. And without the bedjacket, she
thought irrelevantly, it would be the baggage of a
baggage ; and where is the hot-water-bottle ?

" Thank you," she said sternly, and kneeling down
began to rummage in the confusion, using both hands
and trying to make her body bigger, thicker and higher,
so that whatever further horrors her delving exposed
should be hidden from the boy's eyes.

" I think it might be in the other," she said at last.
The hold-all, which was shaped like a twentieth-century
Gladstone bag, closed with a sliding contraption which
gave no difficulty. Intended for last-minute packing it
was at that moment devoted to Penelope's real treasures,
a new typewriter ribbon, a book devoted to historic

costume, Bougère's " Pirates," Grandfather Shadow's
gold watch, the only timepiece which would accurately
record the passing hours when in Penelope's keeping,
and a smudgy snapshot in a silver frame, showing Elsie
and the children on a day's outing at Felixstowe ten
years ago. An odd collection perhaps, but honourable
compared with the other. And at the very bottom, flat
against the flat base of the hold-all, lay the hot-water
bottle. Penelope retrieved it triumphantly and held it out.

He was leaving with it in his hand when Penelope
remembered Miss Dewhurst, Miss Shrewsbury and the
telephone.

" There's a telephone here ? " she asked.

" Sure." He met her eye for the first time and
smiled. " It's in the passage, first door on the right
at the back of the stairs."

Penelope went down. The cats had gone. Twilight
had come and a light had been switched on in the
room opposite the one from which the mad face had
stared. The door was half open and Penelope caught
the sound of a subdued babble of voices ; none of them
sounded English. For the first time she gave a thought
to those who might be her fellow guests.

The door the boy had mentioned opened on a long
dim passage, stone flagged, with walls painted a
villainous chocolate brown. There was nothing in it
except an upturned bicycle and the telephone fixture.
The air smelt of stale cooking and Penelope guessed
that the door at the further end led into the kitchen.

She gave Miss Shrewsbury's number and waited until
a bright, professionally cheerful voice replied from the
end of the line. Then she broke the news about Miss
Dewhurst and found a modicum of comfort both in
Miss Shrewsbury's little murmurs of attention and in
her light-hearted " My word, aren't women a *nuisance* ! "

It sounded as though the agent found nothing funda-
mentally disturbing in this tale of woe, nothing unusual,
nothing insurmountable.

" Well, don't worry," said the bright voice. " I can
fix you up, I've no doubt. I believe actually I know
the very woman, and I have an idea she's on the
telephone. I'll ring her now and ask if she'll meet you
here. Would tomorrow morning do ? "

Penelope considered.

" No. . . ." she said, slowly. " You see, I don't
want to go home until I have somebody there. Look,
I don't want to see her, I don't want any references,
I don't care within reason what I pay or what she's
like. I leave it all to you. You ring me and say
when and where I can pick the woman up. You'll do
that. Oh thank you, Miss Shrewsbury, that's very
good of you. Goodbye." She had almost hung up
the receiver when a sound, as near a shriek as Miss
Shrewsbury's unruffled voice could utter, shrilled out
of it and checked her hand.

" But I don't know where you are ! You say you're
not at home and you don't say where."

" Oh," said Penelope, aghast at this new proof of
her own stupidity, " I'm so sorry. I'm at . . ." she
bent her head, then leaned back, screwing her eyes to
read the number at the base of the telephone.
" Hawberry 1025."

" Thanks," said Miss Shrewsbury. In her neat office
she added the number of the other facts which she
had jotted down while Penelope was talking. " Utter
fool," she said to herself, " how can she expect to keep
anybody ! I'll bet she contradicts herself twenty times
a day."

Penelope was turning from the telephone when it
occurred to her that Caroline, who like everyone else

who knew her, distrusted her driving, would probably ring her home later on in the evening to hear of her safe arrival. Especially was this likely since the snowstorm had blown up. No answer from the Dower House would convince Caroline that her friend was in either hospital or mortuary. Exceedingly pleased with herself for thinking of this Penelope turned back to the instrument and gave Caroline's London number.

" Press Button A," said the impersonal voice as it had done ten minutes earlier. Penelope pressed Button B, and stepped aside hastily, for a shower of coins rattled into the little receptacle intended for rejected offers, and spilled over on to the floor.

At that moment, while she stood there, holding the receiver at arm's length and staring at the pence and shillings and sixpences that danced and rolled round her feet, the kitchen door opened and the boy, with an expression of fury and exasperation upon his face, looked out along the passage.

" Oh," he said, his face gradually calming, but remaining displeased, " it's you." He looked avidly at the money.

" Something's happened," said Penelope helplessly " It just shot out. And . . ." she held the receiver experimentally to her ear, " I haven't got an answer." Which was true, for the girl at the telephone exchange had merely thought, " It's them mad foreigners again," and given her attention to other matters.

" You must have pressed B by mistake."

" Maybe I did." Suddenly she felt cheerful. " In future I shall make a point of pressing Button B."

He grinned, showing white, crooked teeth, and deepening the funny little line which ran in a half-moon round the quirked end of his lips. " I always do," he confessed. " Either it's got something wrong with it,

or else they don't understand, but there's generally
something in it. As a matter of fact I forgot to clear it
last night." His face took on a rueful look, deadly serious
suddenly, and he looked down at the money again.

"Well," said Penelope, "if they're your perks pick
them up. I don't want them. Oh but," she added,
as he scrambled round, obeying her without question
as without delay, "give me back a shilling will you?
It was mine, and I do need it."

"Oh thanks," he said, getting to his feet, selecting a
shilling and handing it over with a beatific smile.
Penelope, holding the dead receiver to her ear said
plaintively, "I can't make anyone hear."

"Better start from scratch again," he said. "Here,
what number were you wanting?" She told him and
he took the receiver, replaced it, waited a second and
then lifted it again. After a moment he reached
backward, "Shilling, please," inserted it, pressed the
right button and then handed her the receiver. Penelope
had been staring into the kitchen which was brightly
lighted and which offered a unique example of still-life.
A laundry basket, so full that the lid was only three-
parts closed stood just within the kitchen door. On
the sloping top of it reposed what could only be a plum
pudding, anyway it was a white pudding basin with
a brownish cloth tied over it ; and sitting on the top
of that, as on a throne, was one of the ginger cats
performing a thorough and fastidious toilet.

But the boy, having handed over the receiver, grinned
cheerfully and dashed away, and there stayed on the
air in the dark dismal passage a kind of radiance, so
that Penelope began describing with unusual vivacity,
the place in which she was staying, adding, " But there
is a rather attractive boy ; so far he has answered the
door, brought up my luggage and promised to fill my

hot-water bottle, and by the flour on his arms just now I rather gather that he's doing some cooking."

She chatted with Caroline until the pips sounded, and then, having no more money with her, rang off hurriedly. Within two seconds the kitchen door opened again and the boy skipped into the passage, throwing a stealthy, backward glance over his shoulder.

"I say," he said, rather breathlessly, "I've been doing a bit of calculating. Nobody's been in that bed since I've been here, that's a month. Whyn't you say you want to go into number four. That's aired, I know."

Without a moment's pause he skipped back into the kitchen again and Penelope heard him say peevishly, "All right. All right. I thought I heard the telephone." And he *was* cooking, thought Penelope, for he had a wooden spoon in his hand that time. The thought went through her head that he was the kind of person she needed ; versatile and cheerful ; and another added itself. Because she had not disputed his claim to largesse of Button B, he was well enough disposed towards her to warn her about that bed. She could not recall a single instance when more deliberate and painful kindness upon her part had returned anything like so generous a dividend. God, she had bought and dressed and concealed a little Christmas tree as a surprise for those ingrate Dewhursts, who were only too obviously willing for her to sleep in damp beds for the rest of her natural life.

She went back into the hall. It was lighted now, but still icily cold. She fidgeted about nervously, pretending that she was waiting to beard Miss Beasley about the change of room. But what to say, what reason to give, she could not think. From the boy's manner she guessed that Miss Beasley was in the kitchen, and when the door into the passage opened at last, she made, almost automatically for the stairs, and was half-way up as Miss Beasley, moving with great dignity, crossed the hall and went towards the room from which the mad woman had stared. She told herself that she was going upstairs in order to ascertain for herself that the bed was damp, that she was not shirking or even postponing an interview which might be awkward. So, upstairs again, she felt inside the bed, and knew, by the clamminess which had gathered around the hot bottle, that she had an incontrovertible cause for complaint. But she knew just how coldly and sceptically Miss Beasley's eyes would regard her; knew how, without saying anything much, she would accuse her guest of ingratitude, fussiness, an almost vulgar regard for comfort. There were people like Miss Beasley, so rooted in their own prejudices, so complacently satisfied with their own personalities that they invested their judgments with a disproportionate importance. After all, thought Penelope, in this case I am the customer; and the customer is always right. So she went over to the suitcase, took up the leaking brandy flask and emptied it in two long draughts. Now, she thought, I'll smoke a cigarette while it sinks in, and then I can face her. For a moment a niggling sense of honesty gibed at her from the back of her mind, accusing her of flying to Dutch courage and attempting to prove that she was afraid of Miss Beasley for the very good reason that Miss Beasley would never need brandy to help her to register a complaint. All right, she said to herself, she may be a better woman, but I wouldn't ever put anybody in a bed like that. Ah, said the critic, but personality isn't what you *do*, it's what you *are*. By that time the brandy had crept about her body; she was warm for the first time in hours, and fired by the memory of the film of damp around the bottle, she stepped briskly downstairs and tapped on the door of the room into which Miss Beasley had vanished.

" Come in," said the headmistressy voice. Penelope opened the door and had just time to take in the vision of the two ladies seated on either side a bright red fire, Miss Beasley knitting, the mad sister fondling a kitten on her lap, when Miss Beasley dropped her knitting and with an expression of surprise mingled with one which asked, how dare you come in here ? rose, swept up the room, through the doorway and into the hall, and took Penelope with her. She closed the door with a decisive little snap.

" That is my private room," she said, without a trace of apology in her voice. " You wanted me ? You should have rung your bell."

" I want to change my room," blurted Penelope, going to the heart of the business at once.

" Oh. That is easily arranged. One would like to know why."

" The bed is damp."

" I find that difficult to believe."

" Unfortunately it is true."

" Well," said Miss Beasley, raising her thick shoulders in a little gesture which was half incredulity and half tolerance and altogether offensive, " you must move, of course." She eyed Penelope with intense disfavour.

" Will you come up and feel how damp it is?" asked Penelope.

Miss Beasley gave a smile which was like the movement of dust under the impact of the March wind.

" There is no need for that. If you can wait until after dinner I will get your things moved. The boy is busy at the moment." She tapped her thumbnail thoughtfully against the edge of the pince-nez. The

mirthless smile moved again over her face. " Of course,
you put me in rather a quandary. I offer you a bed
which to the best of my knowledge is aired ; you say
it is damp. How can I be sure that you will not find
similar fault with any other I offer ? To me, I must
say, all the beds seem alike."

Penelope lost her temper, and with it the last grain
of fear for Miss Beasley.

" Miss Beasley," she said coldly, " you know as well
as I do that a bed which hasn't been used for a month
in mid-winter needs to be aired before anyone sleeps
in it. I'll have my things moved into number four
which was used last night."

A dull red flush, like a stain, crept over Miss Beasley's
face.

" Very well, as you say," she snapped in a voice
which boded no good for someone. She turned away.
Penelope, left standing in the cold hall thought, now
I've done it. I've got *him* into trouble. I'm a mucker
and a muddler, that's what I am. She went up to
her room and sat disconsolately, staring at the bed
which was the cause of the trouble, and smoking
cigarettes, one after the other, until it was seven o'clock
and time to go down to the dining-room.

The boy seemed to have been looking out for her.
As soon as she had opened the door upon what sounded
an intimidating babble of voices and clatter of cutlery,
he was by her side, motioning her deftly into her seat.
He had given her a table near the door so that the
whole of the long room was within her view. There
were fewer guests than the noise warranted, yet more
than the deserted appearance of the hall and corridors
would have led one to expect. They were all, save
one—an extinguished-looking fair girl seated with her

parents—elderly and rather dull seeming. And several were foreigners who said a few English words, like " Good evening," or gave orders to the boy in careful, endearing fashion and then relapsed into their own languages with enthusiasm, seeming to speak more loudly and more quickly than English people would have done, and not allowing the process of eating to interfere with conversation. Penelope identified three as French, two separate couples as German ; another trio left her guessing.

At the table opposite her own Miss Beasley sat in solitary state. She had changed her dress for one of leaf brown with a green sprig raised on it. Pretty stuff, thought Penelope, but spoiled by being made up in the same uncompromising, archaic fashion ; yet there was no doubt that this datedness had a good deal to do with Miss Beasley's impressiveness. Would it do anything for her, Penelope wondered, and if so what about a nice ruff and farthingale ?

The boy had changed too. Indeed he was transformed, he might have been a stage waiter. There was something a little theatrical in the perfection of his tail coat and high stiff glistening collar worn with those spotted trousers and broken shoes, and in the deftness of his movements, in the unhurried speed with which he moved about from end to end, from side to side of the long room.

He brought her a soup-plate of clear grey liquid faintly tinged with green and bearing upon its surface three floating globules of yellow grease. One spoonful told Penelope that it had the taste of water that has been used for washing a greasy pan previously used for onions. She was not, ordinarily, very particular about her food, although she would have said that she liked "things to be nice " ; but tonight her empty

stomach was queasy, and she thought about the cat
sitting on the pudding, and as she thought she saw one
of the Frenchmen, who had reached a further stage of
his repast, lift a bone to his mouth and bite a mouthful
of meat which clung to it. And bones go into soup!
She laid down her spoon. The boy, passing, whisked
the plate away and murmured, " Ah, you have judgment,"
in a voice so soft that Penelope was left wondering
whether she had actually heard the words or imagined
them.

At the end of the room was a service hatch, close by
it a door into the kitchen. To Penelope's eyes that
end of the room had a greater clarity and vividness
than the table before her, and she stared at it as though
into space. She saw the boy lean forward to the hatch,
refuse something, enter into a sharp, violent yet
controlled altercation with somebody on the other side,
and then, abandoning the argument, fling himself
through the door which swung sharply behind him. In
a few minutes he reappeared, walked to the hatch and
took up a plate which he carried straight down the
room and set before Penelope. Looking down at it
she saw that she had been more than generously treated
in the matter of chicken, and she knew, as certainly as
though she had seen him do it, that the boy had gone
into the kitchen and cut the smooth white slices of
breast for her himself. And she remembered, at the
same time, Miss Beasley's question about mutton and
her promise of " beef tonight." Thankfully she ate her
chicken.

" Ginger pudding ? " asked the boy, removing her
plate and speaking as though it were his painful duty
to name the comestible but that he didn't really advise
it, or expect her to accept it.

" No, thank you."

" Cheese ? "

" Coffee ? " His voice was even more dubious. But
Penelope, who had missed her tea chose to ignore the
hint and presently received, in a pretty green and white
cup, some liquid which in colour was indistinguishable
from the soup save that this was opaque instead of clear.

At that moment, just as the boy stood back, having
put down the coffee with a " well, you asked for it "
air, Penelope knew that she was being watched again,
and following the magnetic pull she stared down the
room at the service hatch. The square now framed a
face, the same mad white face which had peered around
the door. The eyes were so sunk in shadows that their
direction was difficult to detect, but she knew, from
the feeling on her skin that they were looking straight
at her. Just then there was a movement from the
table across the room ; Miss Beasley had jerked her
head. The mad face vanished as though someone had
pulled back the head by the hair.

Miss Beasley rose and moved with dignity out of the
room. Penelope, on her way upstairs again, saw, through
an open doorway what was doubtless the communal
sitting-room, a large apartment capable of seating thirty
people upon its assorted chairs and settees ; but there
was no fire, only white painted radiators on each wall.
The whole room had an air of settled, irradicable gloom
which was not dispelled by the presence of Miss Beasley
who was going round patting up cushions and pulling
loose covers into place. Penelope was visited by another
fit of melancholy ; imagine, she thought, people spend
their lives in these anonymous surroundings. She
realised that she had at least always been blessed with
a home, and thought warmly of Elsie, but for whom
she might so easily have been compelled to live in some
place like this, only worse, more squalid. She made
up her mind that she would write something of the

gratitude she was feeling in her next letter to her half-
sister. Elsie would think it sentimental, but one ought
to *say* these things sometimes. And from thinking of
Elsie it was easy to drift into thought . about that
evening when Elsie had been the direct, though doubtless
unconscious, cause of that impulse which had sent
Penelope out in search of independence. And where
had that landed her ? With a nice home of her own
standing empty, with her Christmas-flowering hyacinths
withering unseen, while she sojourned here. Oh damn !
Oh, God send that Miss Shrewsbury would find someone
and telephone her tomorrow.

It was half-past eight when the boy came to move
her luggage. She had removed the wad of typescript,
the box of cigarettes and her dressing gown from the
case and closed the lid.

" I couldn't come sooner," he said. " There's a lot
of washing up last thing."

He lifted the two bags, Penelope with the dressing-
gown over her arm, the papers and the cigarettes under
it, took the typewriter in her other hand and followed
him out of the room, across the passage and up two
steps into another room, which, though smaller, had a
definitely more lived-in atmosphere.

" You'll be all right here," he said. He looked as
though he were trying to remember something. Then
he shot away and came back with her hot-water bottle.

" I'll fill it again. But that bed's all right. Fresh
sheets too."

" I'll fill it, said Penelope, " I found the bathroom.
Thank you for remembering it, though, with all you
have to do."

He made a sound of weary disgust, " And she advertised
for a waiter ! You wouldn't credit the way she described
this place. It's funny really, if you knew what I thought

I was coming to. Still . . ." he shrugged a shoulder,
and as though deliberately dismissing his troubles,
asked : " How long will you be staying ? "

" Oh," said Penelope, " not long. If the weather
. . . and another little matter . . . clear up tomorrow,
I shall go straight home."

" Well," he said, " I'll be here till Saturday. I'll
look after you till then. After that, God help you."

" You're leaving ? "

" I am that. They don't want a waiter here. At least
they need one, and they need a cook, and a charwoman,
and a porter. I can't work myself to death for a couple
of mad women."

" I should say not," Penelope agreed. " What staff
is there, besides you ? "

" A woman makes beds and swabs round a bit in
the mornings. Miss Florence cooks the lunch and
dinner, I do breakfasts and teas. But she's dotty.
It's as plain as the nose on your face—bless you, I
don't mean *your* nose, Miss Shadow, but it is a fact.
She's dotty. The other one, Miss Beasley, won't see
that. So God knows what'll happen when she's left
in the kitchen alone. As she will be. They'll never
get anybody to stay. Nor in the house either except
a lot of poor bloody foreigners, I beg your pardon,
that don't know any better and a few chance people
like you that'll get away as soon as they can and never
come back. It passes me what made a couple of old
school-marms like them think they could run a place
like this. It must have been quite a spot in its time,
run by two Italians, I believe, run properly with all
the things it says on that notice board. But now. . . ."
He made the same sound of disgust. " You didn't
drink your coffee," he said, following an obvious train
of thought.

"Would you?" asked Penelope. They laughed together. He asked, with a conspiratorial air, as though kindly teasing a child, "Could you drink a cup of tea?"

"I could drink four."

"You shall," he promised. He raised his wrist and studied the big gun-metal watch which strapped to it. "She'll have finished poking round down there now. I generally brew a cup about this time. I *can* make coffee too," he added with a touch of pride, "but that poor dotty thing will do it. I'll be back in ten minutes."

Ten minutes gave Penelope time to shuffle out the items which she needed for the night; then the boy was back with the tea. It was hot and fragrant, and there was plenty of hot-water, which was Penelope's simple criterion of good tea.

"Thank you very much," she said. Looking into his face she saw that, although he acknowledged her thanks with a smile, it was an absent-minded one; his eyes were fixed on the box of cigarettes which she had set down on top of the typescript. Sharp memories of the days when the purchase of cigarettes had made a great hole in her budget, when the consumption of an extra one here and there had seemed a major extravagance, flooded Penelope's mind.

"Have a cigarette," she said, holding the box towards him. "Have several. No, no, more. There'll be plenty left for me." She was not satisfied until, grinning, half-delighted, half-protesting, he had a handful. After the gift it was somehow, by Penelope's curious standards, absolutely imperative that she should talk to him for a little while, so that their exchange might be humanised, less a matter of tit-for-tat, you bring me tea and I throw you a cigarette. So, although, as she lifted the box there went through her a sharp desire to escape to the world where Jane Moore, the Woman Pirate, was enjoying her brief, two-year rule of the Caribbean, an escape which could only be made by banishing the boy and sitting straight down to the typewriter, she controlled herself, and lifting her cup, said, consersationally, " You're Irish, aren't you ? "

His face darkened. Penelope, seeing for the first time the expression which he habitually turned upon Miss Beasley and others who displeased him, thought with surprise that an angry, fierce expression was probably as natural to his face as one of gaiety and obligingness. Those thick chestnut brows needed only the slightest contraction to bring them together in a smouldering bar above his eyes, which looked hot and small.

" Yes, I am, by birth," he said, tight-lipped. " How did you know ? "

" I can't really say that I did *know*," said Penelope gently. " It certainly wasn't by your voice, though that has a lyric quality." She put her head slightly on one side and regarded him. " It's just . . . well, I'm a good guesser, perhaps. For instance, down in the dining-room just now, the three by the table by the window are French, and the two couples on either side are German, I could tell that by their talk. But the other three, the little fat man and the woman with the black fringe and the elderly woman with ear-rings, I couldn't identify at all ; and yet, somehow, I think they're Scandinavian. The man isn't the right shape and the woman isn't the right colour and the old lady might be anything ; but I guess Scandinavian. Now, you can probably confirm or contradict that."

" They're Norwegians," said the boy ; and his face said—oh well, if you can guess as well as that it doesn't matter so much your guessing about me.

" And why don't you like being Irish ? " He looked surprised ; looked indeed on the very verge of denying displeasure. Then he changed his mind and said confidentially :

" Well, it's like this. English people don't understand the Irish ; they think there's only two kinds, those they call charming, but actually think don't wash, superstitious, feckless and not to be trusted with anything ; the other kind violent and blood-thirsty with a bomb in every pocket. Do you see ? So either way, if they know you're Irish you don't get on."

" And you want to get on ? "

" Who doesn't ? "

" Ah, indeed," said Penelope, whose vitals still bore the scars of the inroads made by the fox, Ambition. Forming her next question she renounced all hope of working at her story while the tea was good and hot ; she prepared herself for an outpouring of eager dreams. " And what form does your ambition take exactly ? " she asked.

He shied a little, rather a colt seeing a piece of paper wheel in the wind.

" I want to get on," he repeated. " I've tried lots of things, I've been on my own for seven years, since I was thirteen that is. But there's been no future in anything I did. No future and no money."

This is real ; this is actual life, thought Penelope, relegating Jane Moore and her pirates, and settling down, as all writers, either consciously or unconsciously, are forever settling down to suck a vicarious experience, which, unrecognisable, transmuted out of all knowledge will eventually supply a nugget of grist to the ever-turning mill.

" I'd like to hear what you've tried. That is if you'd like to tell me. Sit down, and light one of those cigarettes."

He sat down, easily, quite at home ; and she knew

that he was one of those few people who would be genuinely at home in any place where they were not actually in discomfort or danger.

" I don't know why I should tell you this," he said, " but it is a long time since I talked to anybody. And it isn't very interesting. . . ." And with that introduction he began to unfold, in such vivid phrases and with such economy of language that it was like watching, rather than listening, the story of his short uneasy life. His father was Irish, a schoolmaster, in a small town. He'd married an English girl whom he had met on a teachers' holiday course, and because of this was always " during the time of the Troubles " (he was unmistakably Irish as he spoke the picturesque phrase) suspected of English sympathies. Aware of this he had flung himself with exceptional violence into the ranks of the extremists and had come by his death, " over that bit of business at Marriconal Dock." His mother had died very soon afterwards, " her heart broken " and the boy had fallen to the care of an uncle, his father's brother, a parish priest in the wilds of Tipperary. The uncle was old and set in his ways, his welcome was grudging and his hospitality meagre. " So mean he was, you'd not believe." But apart from this complaint, which, since it had left a record upon the undying memory of the stomach, the boy remembered, he glossed over the time when he was in Tipperary, and when he related that he had run away at the age of thirteen, he spoke with a twinkle of the eye which said, " And why ? Well, I think we won't go into that." Giving his age as fifteen he had taken a job as kitchen boy on a liner bound for Canada. He had stayed there for two years supporting himself by working in restaurants, being errand boy, cleaning windows. At sixteen he had been cook in a lumber camp. " You mightn't think that much experience, but it was. They were rough, and the grub had to be eatable or else. . . ." A sharp bout of pneumonia had put an end to that employment. This watch that he wore was a parting present from the men at the camp. " They said they wouldn't give me a silver one then I wouldn't be tempted to hock it . . . pawn, you know." After leaving hospital he'd taken a job on a grain boat and come back to London. In the last three years he had worked in a garage, sold brushes on commission, touted for a newspaper, " the worst job ever I had," and then, through the influence of an acquaintance who was a waiter, begun to study that art. " I'd have done better to stay where I was, but it's a slow business making the grade as a waiter, so I snapped at their silly advertisement. But I'm leaving on Saturday. Rightly I suppose I should give a month's notice; but I shan't do anything about that. If she likes to sue me, she can, and I shall say just why I left, and that won't do *her* any good. The only thing is . . ." his face which had been steadily regaining its animation, darkened again suddenly, " she can refuse to pay me, and I daresay she will."

" What will you live on then, while you look for another job ? "

" Faith, hope and charity, probably. Actually the telephone has coughed up a little, and my month here took in Christmas, one or two of them gave me a bit. I reckon I shall manage ; I've got about two pounds." His face brightened; so that Penelope found herself looking with astonishment at a person who could face so cheerfully a prospect which would have so much appalled her.

" You seem to have had an exciting life," she said.

" It wasn't. It's funny you should say that ; Joe, he's the one that started me on the waiting, he'd been

on the same job ever since he left school, and he used
to say he envied me. He'd listen all big-eyed when
I told him about the lumber camp for instance. But life
isn't exciting just because you're moving about. People
who stay in one place always have that idea though."

" And you'll get another job as a waiter, I suppose."

" That, or anything else that turns up first. I can't
afford to be choosy. And that's why I shall never get
on. If you've no education, no trade, and no resources
you can't expect to do more than shuffle along." He
rose lightly to his feet. " Oh well, who cares ? I'm
afraid I've been boring you."

" On the contrary you have interested me very
much." She looked at him, a little envious of his youth
and buoyancy, and a little fearful, too. For the time
would come when he would be old, battered and scarred
by life. It seemed a shame, but what could one do ?
The very formlessness of his wish " to get on " defeated
all plans to bring it about ; if he had been twelve
years old and longing for an education, or a grown
man wanting a plot of land to cultivate, or a woman
yearning to show her prowess in a dress shop, Penelope's
mind would have been busy with sums and plans. But
what could one do for a boy like this . . . nothing
except tip him generously and wish him well.

" I might as well fill this again," he said, picking up
the hot-water bottle.

" That's very kind," said Penelope. " You have been
very kind to me."

" Well, I haven't strained myself over it. And you
look as though you could do with a bit of looking after."

Penelope looked up sharply, scenting impertinence ;
but none was there. He had made a simple statement of
fact, and only a fool or a snob could have resented it.
He went out, swinging the rubber bottle, and Penelope's

eyes turned towards the typewriter. It was small, and growing old, for Penelope had bought it with her first royalty, and the cover had had cups of tea stood on it. and they had left rings, and the corners were battered ; but looking at it Penelope saw none of these things. In fact, she did not see the typewriter at all. Staring at her with sun-wrinkled laughing eyes, was the brown-faced woman, Jane Moore, whose name became a legend during her lifetime ; and behind that heartless merry face, behind that taut figure with its swinging colourful skirts, was the blue silken stretch of the sea, the ragged green of the palm trees. The air of the room known as number four changed suddenly, it smelt of salt and blood, was loud with laughter, and curses, and sea-songs and screams of despair.

Moving like one who fears that a train will leave, a friend depart unwittingly, or a trance break without revelation, Penelope snatched off the lid of the machine, set the already typed sheets on the floor at the left of her chair, the fresh paper on the right, grabbed an ash-tray and the box of cigarettes and sat down in the chair, which was of wicker and creaked dismally. Then, with the typewriter balanced upon her knees she bent forward, her fingers ready poised to weave the net which should catch Jane Moore and Ben Williams and Steve Barnes and all the rest of them, and hold them, frozen and glassed in words so that other people could see them too.

When the boy returned Penelope acknowledged his presence with a wordless grunt which might have expressed gratitude or resentment at this disturbance. He tiptoed away.

At that moment Grandfather Shadow's clumsy but reliable timepiece announced that it was ten minutes past nine. It was just on seven hours later when Penelope looked into that yellowed, clearly marked face again.

In the interval she had typed without ceasing, save for a blindly stumbling visit to the bathroom, and twenty-two brief breaks to light a fresh cigarette. It was almost a record, but not quite. Penelope had two working moods. In one the words came slowly, were examined with critical distrust, rejected with scorn or set down with extreme distaste. At such times a fly buzzing mildly in a window eighteen feet away reduced her to blasphemy, brought her to her feet intent upon slaughter, was sufficient to staunch the slow stream of thought altogether. But this difficult mood alternated with another, when, as Penelope admitted, it seemed as though she were taking down, at breakneck speed, the dictation of some other being. At such times no known noise, no physical discomfort could dent her consciousness. Even the deadly faculty of self-criticism was suspended ; and the odd thing was that, despite haste and physical exhaustion, she never made a mistake during those inspired hours. Then she knew all about the people, was with them, one of them ; then every one of her senses was alert and taut ; she saw and heard, she touched, smelt and tasted, the sights, the sounds, the fabrics, the scents and flavours of another, altogether more vivid world. An hour of such experience made up for twelve spent in drudgery, looking up facts, studying maps, or tapping away without that inner guide. And if, in such an hour, she were really disturbed, forced to listen to a request or a complaint, forced by other people's inexorable habits to take a meal or a bath, the snapping of the thread of thought was as painful as breaking a finger. Lately, working in her own home, she had indulged her temperament and let everything go until the mood ended. It ended gently, like a rapidly revolving wheel growing slower and slower until it stopped. Then there was no shock, no sense of loss. Tonight the mood ended at five minutes to four.

The sunshine, the palm trees, and the shining sea were gone. The imposed personality of Jane Moore, so intrepid, so attractive, so resourceful and so evil, sloughed away ; and there was left only Penelope Shadow, aching in every limb, sick from a surfeit of nicotine, very old and very, very tired, and with a dull sense of misdoing.

The gas stove had exhausted its shilling—which the boy had inserted to prevent a further bungle—long ago, and the room was icy. A thick blue haze of smoke had risen to the ceiling and clung there. Stretching herself painfully, Penelope realised for the first time since last evening that she was not in her own house ; her rattling had probably disturbed somebody. It had. The Scandinavian gentleman on one side, the French lady upon the other had, at separate times beaten upon the dividing walls, he with a tobacco box, she with a high-heeled shoe ; but they might as well have tapped upon a gravestone hoping for response. But now, although she had no evidence of neighbourly grievance, Penelope felt it in the air ; and her penitence was also roused by the sight of the ash-tray, long since filled and now squalidly overflowing with stubs and ash.

Cold, weary to the bone, lonely and conscience-stricken, she stood up and stretched her cramped limbs. It was like coming out of a trance ; she felt weak and empty. I'd give a pound for a pot of tea, she thought. But even had she been at home, and still in possession of Miss Dewhurst's services, there would have been no tea at this hour. Heavens, no ! And even if—as she sometimes wistfully imagined—she had been a man, blessed with one of those little wives whose peculiar function is the ministering to inspiration—even then she could hardly have expected tea at four o'clock in the morning. But tea was what she longed for, tea and a plate of little cheese cubes.

Nothing for it but bed, she thought. In her mind she

went through the routine of undressing ; but there was
not enough vitality left in her to face the ordeal of
standing and stripping in that cold room. She pulled
the pillow out and laid it on the quilt. There was no
eiderdown, so she stumbled stiffly across the room and
fetched her fur coat. Huddling under it she lay down and
fell asleep.

At half-past eight the boy knocked loudly on her door,
opened it a little way, pushed something inside and
whispered, " I've brought you some tea. Breakfast is
at nine." She dredged herself up from the deeps of
sleep and thought for a moment that he had, in some
miraculous fashion, divined her longing for tea and was
pandering to it in the middle of the night. She mumbled
at him, but he was gone already, and she turned to the
watch and saw the time. Outside the window the
morning was already grey.

She groaned a little. Her conscience, which did not
share her artistic proclivities and which always sternly
rebuked any deviation from what it regarded as normal
behaviour, started a long lecture, pointing out that she
deserved to feel even worse than she did, sitting up till
all hours, smoking too many cigarettes, going to bed in
her clothes and even forgetting to open the window to
let out the fug. Just because you write . . . it said,
scornfully. Oh shut up, moaned Penelope. She got off
the bed, slid her arms into the sleeves of the rumpled
coat and carried the tea-tray over to the chair which had
been the scene of last night's orgy. The hot tea slipped
revivingly over her parched tongue and throat. It was
warming, it was resuscitating, it was wonderful. And
the boy had brought it, without being asked. The boy
who had, if he were to be believed, to cook breakfast
for a dozen people or more.

Suddenly, as she sat there, looking and feeling like

death, with a mess of ash on one side and a pile of paper on the other, she was visited by as direct a piece of inspiration as any that had gone into her work. The boy would be out of a job on Saturday ; and she had a job to offer. Surely the logical thing to do was at least to offer him employment. And surely he would find it less hard to look after her exclusively than to cook for a camp of lumber-jacks, or be general-utility man in a place like this. And surely she could pay as well as Miss Beasley could.

Her mind ran off into pleasant speculations, like a dog running down a strange path full of intriguing scents. To have that cheerful face meeting one around corners ; to listen to that lilting voice, to chain that willingness to one's own service. Marvellous.

With a frown of concentration between her brows and moving like a robot because her mind was far away, Penelope finished her tea, took a bath, dressed, and made up her face with more care than usual. When she went down to breakfast the room was empty ; but the door to the kitchen stood open, and just on the other side of it, so that the doorway framed them, were Miss Beasley and the boy. Miss Beasley this morning wore a dress of magnificent purple, sobered down by the tortured application of yard upon yard of black silk braid. She was standing very straight and stiff, and regarding with extreme disfavour a dish of something which she held away from her and slightly to the side. The pince-nez were, for once, in position on her nose and the light from a hidden window played upon them.

" It was perfectly fresh yesterday morning," she announced at last, " and if it had been put straight into the refrigerator it would have been perfectly fresh now."

" But I tell you I did put it in the 'fridge ; I put it in straight out of the basket and never went near it till

this minute. It's stinking; it was turning yesterday.
I knew it and asked you twice shouldn't I steam it and
make a fish pie. Didn't I ? "

" You did. And because, knowing my own business,
I refrained from acting on your suggestion, you kept it
in this warm kitchen so that it might be unusable today.
Bates would never give me fish on the turn. He wouldn't
dare. If you had put it——"

" But I tell you I did——"

" Don't shout at me, *please*. Where do I find the
fish ? On a table within a yard of the stove ; and
judging by its condition it has been there ever since it
arrived."

" Do you call me a liar ? With all these cats about ? "
The curious juxtaposition of the two questions made
Penelope smile.

" Here, take it away. Dispose of it and make a
macaroni cheese for lunch instead," said Miss Beasley,
magnificently ignoring both questions and holding out
the dish, still at arm's length, towards the boy. Penelope
watched enchanted. He had begun to untie the strings
of his apron.

" Take it," Miss Beasley repeated. He rolled the
apron into a ball and threw it away from him. Penelope
saw him stretch out an arm and reach, probably from the
back of an unseen chair, his shabby jacket. Without a
word he began to pull it on.

" What are you doing ? " asked Miss Beasley.

" Getting out. Now."

" You can't."

" Watch me," he said. He came through the doorway
into the dining-room. Miss Beasley, looking round a
trifle wildly, bent forward and set the dish away on
something and was following him into the room saying
something about wages, and notice and summonses.

But the boy had seen Penelope, and a second later Miss Beasley saw her too. The boy grinned and skipped forward saying, " I'd forgotten you hadn't had breakfast." Miss Beasley checked herself in mid-speech and put on dignity again like a garment.

" I'll make your breakfast," he said.

" Very well. Do that. Then I'd like to talk to you. Can you spare a moment ? "

" Sure." He went back into the kitchen, slamming the door. Miss Beasley, who had drawn aside as he passed her, advanced slowly up the room and paused by Penelope's table.

" I am sorry you should witness a domestic scene," she said.

" I didn't mind," said Penelope truthfully. Miss Beasley gave her bleak imitation of a smile and walked on.

Penelope looked out of the window. The snow had turned to rain ; the fir trees were dripping like wet umbrellas ; the little summer-house, in full view of this window, looked like a drowned building, viewed through fathoms of water ; to the left of the window a broken gutter spurted a shower into a puddle. If the boy said yes—and it looked rather as though the gods might be siding with her after all—they could get into the car and drive straight home.

He swept through the door, his gait slightly steadied by the tray he carried. He set it down on a nearby table and lifted its contents one by one. A dish of cornflakes, a jug of milk ; a coffee pot, a rack of toast.

" And what to follow ? " he asked. " Bacon ? Eggs, boiled, fried or scrambled ? Tomatoes finished, I'm afraid."

" I don't eat anything else for breakfast," said Penelope. " This coffee smells good."

" I made it." He paused for a second and then

asked, "I suppose you heard the little set-to, just now ?"

"Yes." She dismissed the unprofitable subject. For a moment her mind spun, framing sentences : " I wonder would you care. . . ." " I've been thinking. . . ." " I suppose you wouldn't consider working in a private house. . . ." None of them sounded right. She couldn't say it.

" You're leaving today ? "

" I am."

" Would you like a lift to the main road ? "

Was it her imagination or did the subtlest shadow of disappointment cross his face.

" It'd be a help," he said.

" I'll be leaving in about twenty minutes. Can you be ready ? "

" I've little to pack. I'll put your bags in the car and bring it round, eh ? "

" Please."

He hurried off. Penelope poured a cup of coffee and lifted it to her lips. Suddenly she set it down again and swore softly under her breath. Now, if he said no, she would be homeless again ; she would miss Miss Shrewsbury's promised telephone call, she would have to go into Strebworth, and if she drew a blank at the Agency she would have to spend the night in the town. What a fool !

Then her mood lightened. This was an impossible place anyway. Nothing Strebworth could offer could possibly be worse. Especially now the boy had gone. She cleared up her cornflakes, drank all the coffee, ate one slice of toast and then, after finding and paying Miss Beasley, who was distrait, with staff trouble on her mind, went up to number four to pack. The room was quite clear, sunk back into its vacuous anonymity.

The boy had packed everything, even the nightdress
which she had laid out and not used. Of course, she
thought, I should have thought of that when he said
he'd fetch the bags down. Fool again. She was a
little embarrassed. But she thought suddenly of Jane
Moore who had once said hardily, " Sex is like eating,
a matter of minutes, not twenty-four hours a day.
What'd you think of a chap that never had his mouth
emptied ? " and took heart. If he said yes, he'd
probably see her nightdress many times. She went
down to the car.

He said, holding the door open for her, " Better be
careful. There're places where it's icy under the rain."
Then he walked round, took his seat beside her and
said, " I hope the old battle-axe sees me going off in
style."

Penelope drove carefully out of the gateway where
a great puddle had gathered. Now, now, was the time
to speak. But still the sentences would not frame
themselves.

" Which way are you going when you get to the
main road ? " he asked.

" To the left. Strebworth way."

" Drop me on the corner then. I'll get a lift on a
truck going to London."

The tree-sheltered road seemed very short. The main
road and the corner positively leaped to meet them.
Rather too near the corner Penelope stopped the car.
It was now or never.

" Listen," she said, " don't let me persuade you or
anything. Do what you think best, of course ; but
if you like *not* to go to London and look for a new
job. . . . I mean if you like to give me a trial. . . . I
mean I would most awfully like you to come and work
for me."

"Why, sure," he said; and if she had been less acutely embarrassed she might have detected the relief in his voice "I'd like that. I would indeed."

"But you mightn't. . . . You don't know anything about it, the place . . . or . . . or me. Look, I'll tell you quite quickly. I live by myself in the country. It's fairly big house, but I use only a few rooms. There's a woman who comes every day to do the work, and perhaps it sounds silly that I should want anyone else. But I work a lot. As a matter of fact I write for my living and I'm not very good at keeping house as well. You see, what I want really, is a housekeeper, somebody to look after the place and say what we shall eat and see that the flowers are changed, and cook a little. I've had several women but they've . . . well, they've got ill, or lonely or something. I don't *think* I'm faddy or exacting, and I don't want a lot to eat." He would have spoken then, but she hurried on, determined that this time the prospective inmate of the Dower House should enter prepared for every one of its disadvantages. "It's a lonely place, just a little village and that about a mile away. There's no fun. But the bus runs into Strebworth and I take the car in quite frequently. And I forget rather a lot, especially when I'm busy, and I think some people find that very annoying. Also I like cups of tea at odd times—quite late occasionally. The person who keeps my house has rooms of their own, a free hand in shops, and I pay two pounds a week."

He gave a little laugh. "I'm your man," he said.

"You're sure? It probably won't be as hard as the Plantation House, but it might be duller."

"That doesn't worry me. Gosh!" he said.

A great burden seemed to have rolled from Penelope's mind. She found herself wanting to shout and sing.

She was on her way home, bringing treasure with her.
Suddenly she was aware that she was sitting in the
stationary car, grinning broadly, idiotically into the face
of the boy who was grinning back in the same fashion.
She made a belated grab at her dignity.

"And now," she said, fumbling with the gear lever,
"I think I'd better know your name."

"It's Terence Munce," he said. "Terry."

PART II

FOUR months later, through a countryside of dazzling beauty, with the low sunshine of a May evening gilding the fresh green of the trees and the meadows full of buttercups and daisies and the hedges whitened with hawthorn, Penelope drove towards Strebworth station to meet Miss Caroline Fletcher who was, at last, coming to spend the week-end and taste her hospitality.

This friendship—if such a name could be given to the slightly uneasy relationship between the two women —was some three years old. In the summer following the publication and the success of " Mexican Flower," Penelope had been invited to become a member of the Quill Club. Spurred on by Elsie, yet, like an urged mule, determined to go so far and no farther, she had compromised, not by becoming a member immediately, but by accepting an invitation to the Monthly meeting and dinner ; and there, paralysed by nervousness and as ill at ease as she had ever been in her life, she had met Miss Fletcher, a lady who had for fifteen years enjoyed a well-earned and indisputable reputation as a writer and critic, and whose name was bound to be included in any list, however short, of prominent women-of-letters.

Ordinarily it would have taken a writer of Penelope's calibre, no matter how successful, some time and effort to reach the closely guarded circle within which Miss Fletcher moved and had her being ; but it chanced that on this particular evening Penelope was wearing a blue velvet dress which made her, from a little distance, look very young and pretty, an illusion which her obvious

shyness fostered, and Miss Fletcher had said, in her
crisp, forthright way, " Who's that little shy girl with
the curls ? " Eager, slightly sycophantic voices supplied
the answer. That was Penelope Shadow, author of the
best seller, " Mexican Flower."

" That can't be true," said Miss Fletcher, studying
Penelope from under massive brows. " Penelope Shadow
wrote " The Cavalier " years ago. A damned good
book, better than this they're making such a fuss over.
And that's a mere child."

" Well, she's down as Penelope Shadow," said someone,
consulting a list.

" Bring her here and let me see for myself," said
Miss Fletcher.

It so happened that Penelope, hitherto immured at
Melbury, and a partaker of Elsie's Sunday paper, which
was not of a literary character, had never heard of
Miss Caroline Fletcher ; and being already nervous and
terrified past all reason, was not in a condition to note
the solemn character of the introduction. All she knew
was that, in this sea of strange faces, amid this welter
of loud confident voices, this parade of clothes exotic
or eccentric, she had been blessed by an introduction
to a woman who looked sensible and kind, who seemed,
even by the Rectory standards, to be sound and respectable, and who spoke in a direct rather homely fashion.

A few observers, better informed than Penelope, who
knew that Caroline Fletcher was neither kind nor
homely, watched with some amazement, the result of
the introduction. Penelope was like a small drifting
vessel coming at last to safe anchor. With glasses of
the famous Quill Sherry in their hands the two women
retired to a seat in a corner and began to talk. Miss
Fletcher prefaced a remark with " Child . . ." and
Penelope, opening her grey eyes a trifle wider said :

" I'm not a child. Good God, I'm thirty-five."

Secretly agog to know what preservative atmosphere
so old an innocent could possibly have been living,
Miss Fletcher drew out, by her own subtle means, the
simple story of Penelope's past. Penelope, with nothing
to conceal, willingly related the story of her days ;
and, because she was aware that it was a dull and
uninteresting story, took pains to set it out, as it were,
with a little humour, with the small vivid tricks of
phrasing which her readers knew and loved. Before
the evening was over Miss Fletcher was enchanted, not
with the pretty young prodigy whom she had at first
taken Penelope to be, but with the odd, contradictory,
unpredictable person that she really was. How anyone
could be at once so simple and so profound, so unworldly
and so frivolous, so innocent, yet so unshockable, roused
Miss Fletcher's jaded sense of amazement.

At the end of the evening she invited Penelope to
her flat. And perhaps, when a few weeks later, Penelope
set about house-hunting, she had in her mind the vision
of a humbler, more rural version of that combination
of living-and-working place. But at the time she
viewed Miss Fletcher's luxurious apartments, her big
desk, her rows of books, the careful attention to every
detail that would make work easy and pleasant, without
any personal feelings at all. And that further endeared
her to Caroline who had known envy from so many
women, and from men too. Like Elsie, Miss Fletcher
realised that Penelope was unique ; unlike Elsie she
felt no sense of responsibility for her, so she was free
to enjoy that uniqueness to the full.

Penelope, of course, learning later the identity and
the reputation of her nice, new, kind, homely friend,
suffered a shock from which she never recovered. The
shyness which should have been hers at the moment

of introduction fastened down belatedly and incurably.
To the end of time she would be a little frightened of
Miss Fletcher, though she should shower her with
kindness, appear genuinely fond of her, even review
her books favourably. And that was why, though
Miss Fletcher had often hinted that she would like to
see Penelope's house, she had never been invited during
the days of Mrs. Grant, Miss Slater, Mrs. Meadows, the
slut, or Miss Dewhurst. Penelope, who had three times
in three years been Caroline Fletcher's petted, pampered
guest, knew that she could only face the ordeal of
acting as Caroline's hostess if she were backed up by
the certainty that the house would look nice, the food
be eatable and the behaviour beyond reproach. Even
during the reign of the competent Mrs. Meadows there
were things which Penelope felt would be bound to
catch and shock Caroline's critical eye.

But now, driving to meet the incoming London train,
she was full of pleasant confidence. With Terry in
the house nothing could possibly go wrong. From the
kitchen where Terry was cooking a dinner fit for a king,
to the spare bedroom with its great bowl of stiff tulips
on the bureau, the Dower House was in apple-pie order,
and something unregenerate and very feminine in
Penelope's heart was looking forward to showing Caroline
that even in the country, even with the minimum of
staff, things could be as comfortable and orderly as in
the luxurious service flat off Baker Street.

For Penelope had secured a treasure. There was no
other word for it. She had won not only a housekeeper
who could cook, and a cook who could housekeep, she
had, all in one person, a nurse, a mentor, a chauffeur,
a chambermaid, butler and steward. Without any
unpleasantness at all Terry had put Mrs. Paine upon
her mettle, so that the house was really clean ; and he

had similarly inspired Old Rogers who for three summers
past had been postponing quite essential jobs in the
garden. How had he done it ? By drinking cocoa
with the one, beer with the other ? Or was it merely
the force of example? Did his own energy, his almost
incredible passion for serving Miss Shadow shame these
two amiable but lethargic creatures ?

The train came in just as Penelope reached the
platform, and at the first sight of Caroline's massive
figure alighting from a first-class carriage, all the little-
girl-gaucherie in her came to the surface. She forgot
that she had found this woman pleasant and homely
and kind ; she remembered only the world-wide
reputation, the great two-volume book on the history
of the drama which Caroline had just published, the
respect with which she had heard eminent people address
her, the eminent people themselves whom she had met
in the Baker Street flat. She thought of the hours
ahead . . . would Caroline like the country or find it
dull ? What would she think of the little dinner-party
tomorrow night ? There would be no one there whose
name had ever been heard of outside Essex. Had
she been wise to take Terry's word about the wine ?
All these thoughts went through her head as she
advanced and held out her hand towards her guest.
Caroline, reminded of the first moment when she had
seen Penelope, and thinking anew what a pretty little
thing she was, laid her large, perfectly manicured hand
on her shoulder, pulled her closer and kissed her.
Penelope felt better—of course, Caroline was nice.
Caroline was her friend. She smiled and said happily,
" It was nice of you to come. I am so glad to see you."

From that moment, it seemed, the week-end was a
success. Caroline liked the house and garden, and
said so in a voice which was unmistakably genuine.

Even the dinner-party seemed to go with a swing. Penelope's guests, the Willises—now moved into their brand-new house behind the tree belt, Babs and Derek Morrison, and a young lawyer, Oliver Watling, who had done some business for Penelope and had developed a rather school-boyish infatuation for her, seemed to be inspired by the presence of the famous Caroline Fletcher so that Penelope, who had secretly feared that they would seem dull and a little parochial, had a bad fit of conscience and accused herself of disloyalty and intellectual snobbery.

And hovering in the background all the time was Terry—who must, Penelope reflected, be working like a black to have cooked and served such a meal with only Mrs. Paine to help him—cheerful, efficient, unobtrusive and yet so palpably " on her side " that the very thought of him gave her confidence. It was a good evening and Penelope loved everybody until Babs Morrison said, " Couldn't you bring Miss Fletcher over to our place tomorrow, Pen, dear ? " And Penelope had a vision of Babs hastily assembling a party of those of her friends who would enjoy meeting somebody " famous," and she remembered that she herself had never liked anyone whom she had ever met in Babs' rather too-carefully-restored house and doubted whether Caroline would either, so she said, without giving the matter a moment's thought, " I'm sorry, Babs, but we've planned our day. I think Caroline would like to see Selberswick. We're taking a picnic lunch."

" You could come home by our place and dine. Any time you like," said Babs in her persistent way.

" Too tired," said Penelope. " Thanks all the same."

After that the evening was good again. It was almost twelve o'clock when Penelope went to the door and watched the three drive away. She stood for a moment sniffing, with a child's keen perceptive sense, the fragrance of green things growing in the warm night. Then, turning, she became aware that another scent was being faintly borne through the house. It smelt of cooking. Terry must have left something on the stove.

She crossed the hall, passed along the short passage and opened the kitchen door. She was so sure that the room would be empty that her hand was in position to press on the switch and flood the place with light. But the kitchen was lighted, and occupied. A big pot was bubbling on the stove and on the table sat Terry, swinging his legs, smoking a cigarette and studying the back page of the evening paper which Oliver Watling had brought in with his hat and left behind on the hall table.

He jumped off the table when he saw her.

" Did you want something ? " he asked with his ready smile.

" I thought I smelt cooking. I wondered if you'd left something on the stove."

" Sure I did," he said, jerking his head towards the pot. " A ham. You said something about a picnic tomorrow and I thought you'd like it."

Such thoughtfulness !

" That was very nice of you, Terry. Actually, though, I'm not sure about it. It was an excuse really."

" I see," he said, with understanding. " All the same it'd be a good idea. Why, if it was a day like this it'd be warm enough to swim."

Penelope laughed. " I can't see either Miss Fletcher or myself swimming," she said.

" Why not ? It's grand."

" You like it ? "

" I do."

Her gaze had lighted upon the side table which stood
under the kitchen window. Good heavens, he had
found her old picnic case, relic of happy days with
Elsie and the children. Where had he discovered that ?
She herself could not have found it for any wager,
was not even aware that she had brought it from
Melbury. He was a marvel. For there it was, everything in it clean and shining ; the sandwich boxes
stood on their sides, the thermos bottles upside down,
draining. Close at hand lay a clean table-cloth and two
snowy napkins.

Suddenly the pathos of it struck her. He threw
himself so completely into her plans. And he wasn't
going. And he liked swimming.

" We will go," she said. " And Terry, if you don't
mind, I'd like you to come too and drive us. Then
we can sit at the back and talk. You know how it is
when I try to drive and talk."

He looked pleased. " But you don't like anyone to
drive you," he reminded her.

" I think I could bear you to do it. Anyway I'll
try," she said.

The next day was perfect ; so was the drive through
the miles and miles of rich flat countryside with its
buttercup meadows, its green woods, its little villages
with cottage gardens full of flowers and the occasional
chiming of church bells. Selberswick was perfect too,
romantic ; for the sea was encroaching there, and there
were three churches and a whole town under the water.
Penelope and Caroline talked about the days when it
had been a flourishing place, doing a great trade in
wool with the Continent ; and of the later days when
it bolstered its tottering fortunes with smuggling. The
lunch was good too and included several things not

usually taken on picnics, things which Terry had put in " for a surprise." And there was Terry himself, young, good-looking and attentive. He might have been Caroline's son, Penelope's nephew, with just a shade better manners than sons and nephews are wont to display. And Penelope was very glad that at the end of his first month with her she had given him some money and told him to buy some clothes.

After lunch he asked Penelope how much longer she wished to stay, and then took himself off to find a place to swim.

" You'll be all right ? " he asked.

" My dear boy, of course," said Penelope, and the *dear* was affectionate, not patronising or automatic.

" He's sweet, isn't he ? " she said, following his retreating figure with her eyes.

" He's all right, I suppose," said Caroline non-committally.

Penelope started as though she had been stabbed by a pin. She narrowed her eyes and looked earnestly into her friend's broad, powerful face.

" All right," she repeated. " What on earth do you mean by that ? "

" Just that," said Caroline, meeting the earnest glance with one of candour. " You mustn't spoil him, you know, Penelope. Young males are uppitty creatures."

" You mean bringing him today ? "

" No. No, my dear, I hadn't given that a thought. It was rather . . . it was . . . well," she hesitated in a manner which would have amazed many people who did not know her softer side. " You rather let him see how much you depend on him, Penelope. That makes people take advantage, you know."

There, she thought, she had said it. She had hoped she would find courage to do so before she left, because,

Portville Free Library
Portville, New York 14770

before she had been an hour in the Dower House, it
had seemed to her to be something which ought to be
said. But she cursed herself for a busybody and a
meddling fool as she watched the pink colour flare into
Penelope's cheeks.

" He's very useful. In fact he's unique. And you
want to keep him, don't you ? " she asked gently. " So
you mustn't let him get the notion that you couldn't
do without him."

" But I couldn't," said Penelope. " Good God,
Caroline, if you knew what I've been through with
women ! " I can guess, thought Caroline, if what I
have seen is a fair sample of how you treat your servants.
Aloud she said : " Oh, nonsense. Nobody's indis-
pensable, Pen. If you get to thinking that you'll be
like Queen Victoria and her John Brown. You'll have
him telling you your bonnet's cruiked."

" I wouldn't mind that—if it were," said Penelope,
laughing.

And yet she *did* mind, when, on the drive home,
Terry said :

" It's turning chilly. You ought to close that window
and put on your coat."

Almost without thinking Penelope began to wind up
the window ; wound it, with her usual inexpertness,
down, and saw the long tweed-clad arm shoot outwards
and backwards. Half standing in his seat Terry wound
the window up.

" I shan't want my coat now," Penelope said. And
almost immediately she became conscious of cold, so
that she began to think longingly of the soft fleecy
garment, and the snug caress of its collar. Oh, if only
Terry hadn't mentioned it. And Heaven send that he
wouldn't mention it again. But he did, of course. He
said, with the good humour that bridged so easily the

supposed gulf between employer and employed, the good humour that took no note of the presence of the third person, " You know you'll be a winter-green case tomorrow."

She remembered, with a pang of shame and penitence, that time in February when her shoulder had been so stiff and painful that she could not type a word ; and Terry had, without making any bones about it, rubbed out the stiffness and the pain with a liniment of winter green and menthol. She could feel again the firm, yet gentle pressure of his thin hard hand. Suppose she should be stiff tomorrow, what a fool she would feel ! Annoyed with herself for minding Caroline's possible criticism, and for being so vacillating, she snatched up the coat, shrugged her way into it and then sat for a moment, looking and feeling like a sulky child. She saw that Terry, through the driving mirror, had flashed her a look of amused approval. It made her angry ; not with him, but with herself. Surely it showed a hideous weakness of character that she should resent his care for her merely because it was observed.

Nevertheless, throughout the rest of the week-end, and for a time after Caroline's departure, she was conscious of a new feeling in her attitude towards the boy. She began to watch herself, wondering. She could imagine that Caroline had gone away thinking, poor little Pen, she has to be looked after and since there is no one else to do it she depends on her houseboy for attention. She could imagine people saying, " He even tells her when to put her coat on." She began to see herself as a doting, silly old lady. The clear natural spring of her gratitude to him for his services, her delight in his looks and in his unvarying cheerfulness, was poisoned by this self-distrust. Once or twice she even attempted a mild snub of which she was instantly

ashamed. And then she took comfort from the thought
that the whole trouble lay in the fact that for a moment
Caroline had forced upon her a conventional view of
the situation. Caroline had said, " Young males are
uppitty creatures," and almost implied that old maids
of between thirty-five and forty were silly ones. Such
sweeping generalisations were wrong. Other lonely
women, even Queen Victoria, might let themselves be
bossed by any man who chanced to be handy ; but
she and Terry were different. Two people. Two people
whose very different temperaments and accomplishments
enabled them to live together, in fact fitted them for
the special position they held.

With that thought she put the problem away from
her, and, without much difficulty, forgot all about it
in following the now declining fortunes of Jane Moore,
the woman pirate.

June slipped away and July came, with the scent of
hay all about the countryside, with the corn in ear
and growing tall, with a second crop of roses in the
garden of the Dower House. On the third Tuesday
in this month—a day she was long to remember—
Penelope finished the novel. Jane Moore, with all her
sins upon her head, died wretchedly, but not without
a certain grandeur of fortitude, on a stone floor of a
prison cell in Port of Spain, and the story was ended.

It was nine o'clock when Penelope rose from her
desk. The tops of the trees in the garden were still
awash in golden light, but in the beds the big white
daisies, the larkspur and delphinium spikes, the velvet
snapdragons and the roses were already losing their
colours, retreating into the greyness of the dusk. She
stepped out through the french windows and walked
to a seat at the end of the path, a white seat set against
a thick dark hedge of clipped box. As always when a

story was ended, she felt emptied, a little lonely ; and she wished that Terry were home. But often during these summer evenings, he went out after dinner, and usually Penelope did not mind. He was always home before it was dark, and it was only right that he should have some life of his own.

Penelope sat still, breathing the scent of her roses through the scent of her cigarette, thinking a little about Jane Moore and a little about other matters and planning that when Terry came home she would tell him that the story was finished, and tell him, what was no less than the truth, that she had finished it earlier and with greater ease because she had been able to concentrate upon it, leaving everything else in the world to him. And she would invite him to join her in drinking her nightcap of whisky ; because although people would say that you shouldn't drink with your servants, she had done it before, and no harm had come of it ; and besides, although she was enlightened enough to drink anything she fancied and could pay for, there remained, as a residue of the Rectory days, a sneaking feeling that whisky was really more a man's drink than a woman's and it was, somehow, a little awkward not to share everything with someone who was as kind and as valuable as Terry.

The shadows deepened. The last bird calls began to die away. A little breeze sprang up, ruffling and cooling the earth without chilling or disarranging it. Penelope looked at her watch. It was just on ten o'clock. Nearly dark. She must go into the house. She half rose from the seat and then sat back again. She had left it too late. The house had changed from a possession, a happy place where one lived and ate and slept and had become a menacing, dark hulk, the abode of darkness and mystery, an alien territory not to be

approached without the help of a friendly human
presence, or a bright and friendly light.

She sat aghast, staring through the gathering darkness
at the house which she dare not enter. She felt such
self-scorn that she was almost sick with disgust. She
hated herself, seeing, as an unsympathetic stranger
would have seen it, the absurdity, the grotesque
absurdity of her position. If she had stayed indoors
and made a light she could have waited happily enough
until Terry came in, even if he delayed, as he had done,
until almost eleven. And now she had only to go in
by the door and switch on the light in the hall, cross
it, go to her study and switch on the light there—no
step need be taken in darkness. But she knew, only
too well, having argued out such a question, and
occasionally acted upon the reasonable argument, how
as the light went on in hall or room the place would
change, but just too late, settling back into normality
and ordinariness, but not soon enough. She would
have caught a flash of what happened in empty houses
in the dark; she would have seen the shadows shape
and retreat. It was no good. She couldn't go into
the house. She must wait until Terry came home.

Almost immediately her self-hatred gave way to
febrile irritation and maudlin self-pity. Why couldn't
he come home a little sooner? Why did she allow
herself to get into this position? She could afford two
people, or three, to live with and work for her. Her
ideas were too modest, that was what was wrong.
Probably lots of women hated being in houses alone,
and took care never to be, and so arranged that their
mental infirmity was never suspected. Tomorrow she
would engage two maids, and they could alternate their
nights out with Terry's. She would never be alone
again. But even as she realised the childish thought

she imagined what life would be like then . . . quarrels, jealousy. Oh dear, she and Terry had been so happy. If only he had come home at dusk ! If only she had stayed inside the house and built up a safe cell of lighted occupation within that black bulk !

And now the garden was not much better. Penelope was learning that to forsake the house for the lighted streets of a town was a very different thing from forsaking it for a lonely tree-encircled garden. She began to think about old primæval forests ; she became conscious of the thick hedge behind her, of the black shadows under the beech tree. She began to think about watchful eyes ; to imagine that she could hear stealthy movements. This was madness. God, she was going crazy. Oh, Terry, please, please come home. She jumped to her feet and ran to the middle of the lawn where at least there were no shadows. She stood there trembling.

Terry's first loud call did little to comfort her. It was a loud, vague shout and the voice was not instantly recognisable. But in less than a moment the door into the hall of the house opened, and against the light within she could see Terry's unmistakable figure. He called again, " Cooee," and then, leaving the door open, came running on to the lawn.

" I'm here," she said, as soon as she had drawn a steadying breath. All her fears fled away. She walked towards him as casually as though she had just left the house for a breath of air.

" What are you doing out there in the dark ? " he asked. And still his voice sounded thick and strange.

" Just sitting and thinking."

" But it's dark," he repeated. As he spoke he put his hand on her arm, above the elbow, just below the little puffed sleeve of her dress. " You're frozen, you silly." He kept his hand on her arm ; and as he spoke she realised what was the reason for this familiarity and for the queerness of his voice. A strong odour of spirits was borne towards her on his breath.

She stepped to one side, drawing her arm away, and said mildly,

" Terry, you've been drinking."

" Yes, I've been drinking. And I've been in a fight. But," he added hastily, " I'm not drunk. Don't go thinking I'm drunk, because I've got something to say to you and you mustn't think I'm drunk."

" Let go my arm then and come into the house. What have you done ? Hurt somebody ? "

" Yeah, I hurt him. But not enough. That won't stop what they're saying."

" Would you fall over if you let go my arm ? " she asked drily. He said, " Sorry," and dropped his hand. She walked ahead of him into the house. Five minutes before she had been gibbering with senseless terror ; now, followed by a boy of whom she really knew very little, a boy who was drunk, a boy who had just laid a familiar, if not exactly disrespectful hand upon her, she was perfectly calm and cool. And now there was her study exactly as she had left it, with nothing to suggest that had she entered it a little earlier, alone, it would have been a place of terror.

She turned and faced him. There was a lump, like a small egg, on his jaw to the left of his chin, and a long, thin, jagged cut with bloody edges running from his right eyebrow to the edge of his bright hair. Out of this altered face his eyes shone, narrow and furious.

" Now," she said, seating herself at her desk and folding her hands on the edge of it. " Tell me what you've been up to."

" I told you. I got in a fight."

"What about?"

"You," he said, with venom in his voice. "Did you know that people were talking about us?"

"No. What are they saying?"

"Filthy things. Can't you imagine? Can't you guess? About you and me." His voice rose, the tone becoming shrill, the words remaining thick and slurry. "Being here alone together and that old faggot, Mrs. Paine, God damn her soul, saying about the clothes I have new and the time I rubbed your stiff shoulder. You said it. . . . I well recall your saying that your shoulder was better after Terry rubbed it. What'd you want to say that for? So that Ginger Jaggard, the fat gutted ——, could say what he did this evening." He narrowed his eyes still more and thrust his face towards her. "Don't you mind? Don't you care about what they're saying?"

"Not very much," said Penelope Her traitorous faculty of self-criticism reminded her that she had minded, a little, about Caroline's remarks; but these were ignorant people whom, in her heart, she despised, though she occasionally wrote about such people touchingly. "But I can see that you mind, Terry. And we must do something about it, of course."

"What?" he asked. His battered face was white and small with emotion; the edges of the cut were beaded with blood. His eyes looked anxious as well as angry.

Penelope stood up.

"First," she said, "You must bathe your head. And while you do that I'll make some coffee, if you show me where the things are. Then we can talk. I meant to have a little talk with you this evening anyway. I've finished my book."

He looked at her a little doubtfully, but without

argument took her into the kitchen, showed her the
coffee-making things and went away. In a short time
he was back, his hair wet and smooth, a long strip of
adhesive tape decorating his brow. Some soberness had
returned to him. He said, a little sheepishly, " I'm
sorry, showing myself to you like that, and blurting
the whole thing out. But I was damned angry."

" Quite right you should be," said Penelope. " I
suppose *I* ought to be biting the carpet. After all it's
my reputation and even the reputation of an ageing lady
is a tender matter."

" Don't say that," he said. " Don't say you're ageing.
You're in your prime."

" Thank you, Terry. That was very gallant. Drink
your coffee."

There was silence in the kitchen for a little time,
then Penelope said, " It's curious, but I was thinking
about making some changes this very evening."

He looked up sharply. It was as though she had
threatened him in some way.

" I can easily get somebody else to live here. You
work too hard anyway, Terry. Which would you rather
I looked out for, help in the kitchen with the cooking,
or a parlourmaid ? "

His face went dull and heavy, so that for a moment
Penelope thought that his cut was not so superficial
as it looked and that a kind of delayed shock was
stunning him.

" So that's the remedy ? " he asked.

" Can you think of a better one ? "

" I could leave. Go away."

She was too much appalled by the idea to notice
how carefully he watched the result of this suggestion.
Her mind plunged backwards into memories of the
days before she had Terry. Horrible ! She had known

then that they were horrible ; now, after testing the sweets of perfect willing service she would find the old state of things unendurable.

" Oh no, Terry. You mustn't do that. I couldn't bear it. Really I couldn't. I'd rather anything than that you should go."

" It'd be best, though. In fact I've thought about it a lot. Maybe it was a mistake for me ever to have come."

" Why ? Haven't you been happy ? Is it because of this silly chatter ? "

He looked at her again. His expression had altered and become that of a man who measures carefully with his eye the height of an obstacle, the width of a gulf, before bracing himself for a leap. He said slowly, " I've been perfectly happy, but for one thing ; I'd be happy to stay with you for ever, but for one thing. And that's not the chatter, that only angers me because it reflects on you. . . ."

" What is it then ? What is it, Terry ? " She repeated the question because he hesitated to give his answer. He hesitated for a further minute and then said :

" I happen to be terribly in love with you."

She had never been so much surprised in her life. She was dizzy and breathless with it. Balaam, when his ass turned and addressed him, was not more taken aback. And mingled with the surprise were other feelings ; a thrill of excitement ; a touch of gratified vanity ; an uprush of tenderness ; above all a sense of responsibility. It was the latter which made her say, with a brisk composure which astonished her,

"Nonsense, Terry. You don't know what you're saying. You admitted just now that you'd been drinking. We'll forget that you ever said it and go to bed now and talk over our plans in the morning."

She made as though to rise from her chair, but before she could do so he had crossed the space between them in a few long strides and stood looking down at her, fury in his face.

"Don't talk to me like that," he said. "Be angry if you like, order me out ; but don't talk as though I were a child or an idiot. I know what I'm saying. I say I'm in love with you. I've been in love with you since the first day I saw you. What d'you think has kept me here ? Why d'you think I got in this fight tonight ? Oh, hell, I know all about our positions and our ages. I know that to you I'm nothing but a glorified kitchen scab, but all the same I'm a man and you're a woman and I'm telling you, I love you."

Bewilderment and consternation had wrinkled Penelope's brow, so that with her small triangular face, her wide innocent eyes and ruffled hair she looked like a fluffy kitten. And it was rather as though a harassed kitten were mewing when she said :

"Oh dear. I never suspected. . . . Are you sure you mean this, Terry ? Or is it just because we get on well together ? You're very young you know . . . and inexperienced."

He said sullenly, "I've made a fool of myself. I'd better get out before I do worse. I can't stay here anyway, after this ; even if that filthy talk wasn't going the round."

"You mean leave me ? "

"What else ? " Again he threw her a calculating glance. Then he said angrily, "Damn all money ; and damn the day I went to work for you. If I'd been a garage hand still and fallen for you like this, it'd have been awkward, but not ridiculous." He seemed to be on the verge of tears.

"I don't think it's ridiculous, Terry. And I . . .

please believe me . . . I'm really very fond of you.
And I'd have been just as taken aback to hear—well,
what you've just said—from anybody. Honestly I
should."

It was a faltering little speech, but utterly true. Miss
Shadow had written pages and pages about love, and
about passion, and about marriage ; but she had never
thought about these things from a personal angle at
all. They were things that happened to other people.
She had great difficulty in realising that here she was,
in her own kitchen, having an imaginary experience
made real before her eyes, taking part in the kind of
scene which she described so well though she had never
known it, never expected it, never even hoped for, or
shrunk from it. And now that it had been made real
she could neither run away from it nor leave it to
someone else to handle. She looked helplessly towards
Terry, who, for six months, had been holding all realities
away from her ; and she was frightened of what she
saw. Terry seemed to have changed from a familiar
tried friend into a threatening stranger—and all because
he had said, " I love you." Something must be done
about it. And God knew she must do or say something
now, at once, to make him feel better. After all, it
wasn't a crime to tell a woman you loved her, even if
she were years and years your senior and happened to
be your employer.

It was kindness moving through bewilderment which
sent Penelope across the kitchen and made her lay her
hand on Terry's shoulder. She was about to make a
trivial, comforting, time-gaining speech and send him
off to bed and go to her own room and try to think
things out clearly and leisurely ; but before she could
speak, something had happened. At the touch on his
shoulder he seemed to become mad. He put his arms

round her and clasped her so tightly that for a moment Penelope was uncomfortable, alarmed, inclined to resist him. Then he bent over her and began to kiss her. And Penelope was lost. Feelings and instincts which she had never dreamed of possessing rose in a great swelling flood. She was no longer conscious of the pressure of his clasp ; she tightened her own hold upon him. She could feel the separateness of her mind and body seeping away, pressing on towards the final act of unseparateness ; and at last, weak and shaking, frightened by her own feelings she said, " Please, Terry, let me go. Let me get my breath."

He released her and she laid a hand on the edge of the kitchen table for support. He looked at her, still a little uncertain, but with a certain arrogance peeping through the uncertainty.

She said unsteadily, " I think I do love you, Terry. If . . if you feel the same way in the morning . . . I think we'll have to get married."

And with that bold assertion she slipped hastily away, up the stairs, and into her bedroom where she locked the door. So she missed the expression of calculating triumph which, despite his efforts to repress it, dawned on the boy's face at her final word. It was a natural expression, the result of inevitable feeling. After all, one likes six months of hard labour to bear some result.

PART III

EXACTLY two years after her amazing marriage, Penelope
sat down to her typewriter to begin a new book. She
spread her small blunt fingers over the keys of the
machine and held them there for a moment without
moving them, while through the brain which lodged
within the curly skull, a medley of thought went milling.

Two years; and she hadn't written a word since
that night when she had finished " Jane Moore " and
Terry had said that he loved her and she had surprised
herself by falling in love with him. Where had they
gone, those two bright slippery years ? And how much
was she changed from the Penelope Shadow who had
covered this machine, sorted the last pages and wandered
into the garden on that July night ? She tried to
answer the two questions. The two years had been
spent in gaiety ; she and Terry had made long stays
in London, had been to France and Switzerland and
Austria, had spent six months in America, visited scores
of theatres, dined in many famous restaurants. She
herself had bought heaps and heaps of new clothes,
all a little juvenile in pattern—but that suited her ;
and begun to have her hair dyed—and that suited her
too. And there had, of course, been intervals of love-
making.

Now here she was, and it was July again, and she
was sitting down to her typewriter and Terry had gone
to the Newmarket Races. The arrangement suited
Penelope perfectly. For a year, or perhaps a little
more she had enjoyed her idleness, reflecting sometimes
upon the words of Shakespeare in Clemence Dane's

play about him, " I am to live, not write," and flattering
herself that—although she was no Shakespeare—she
would write the better for the experience of living and
loving and being loved. That must be true, mustn't
if ? Shakespeare had said so—at least not he himself,
but Clemence Dane, which was almost as good. Only
it shouldn't be " live, not write," it should be " live,
and write," because for her, for Penelope Shadow who
was only Mrs. Munce on formal occasions, to live was
to write. And that was why she was perfectly happy
to have Terry, and all the disturbing influences that
hung around him, out of the house for the whole day
while she sat down to get into words the things she
had learned in two years.

She withdrew her fingers and took up and opened
the shabby little notebook in which she did her
preliminary scribbling. To anyone else the pages would
look like a mass of childish cyphering ; but she knew
all about it, what page to turn to and what the dis-
connected words and doodles and phrases meant.

Miss Shadow had already informed her publisher that
she was engaged upon a book about Queen Elizabeth ;
and the shabby little notebook was crammed with facts
and figures. But the page to which she turned on this
bright July morning was empty save for a scribbled
sentence, " I know why she never married," and two
lines drawn one above the other. Resting her head on
her hand Penelope studied the page. Then she shut
her eyes and meditated. She had written that sentence
long ago—on what people would call her honeymoon ;
and there was a great deal of hidden meaning behind
the simple words. Now, two years later, she knew that
the flash of intuition which had made her scribble that
sentence had been sound and true. And because of
it Miss Shadow was going to write down, oh, very

cunningly, in fictional form, beautifully decorated and
not the least bit dull, a vindication of the Virgin Queen's
claim to virginity. For on the evening when she had
scribbled those words Penelope Shadow had known
beyond possibility of doubt that though Elizabeth's
father might go to bed with at least six women—
probably more—and remain King of England, his
daughter, being a woman, could never have taken any
man to bed and remained the ruler that she was. There
was the one stark fact, acceptable if you were loved,
and hateful if not, which women had to face ; and
there was the prime fact which marriage had taught
Penelope Shadow.

She knew, even as she settled down to her own job,
in her own house, that she was not her own woman
in the same way that she had been up to the moment
when Terry had kissed her. Even then it had not been
entirely too late ; she could have sent him away ; and
a kiss might have been forgotten in time. But the
ultimate possession was a horse of a very different
colour. And so, in a book about Queen Elizabeth, dead
these three hundred years and more, Penelope Shadow
was going to tell the world that once she had been the
mistress of her small kingdom, with a faithful servitor ;
and that now she was just a woman in love. Oh, she
was as certain as though she had been there, that
Elizabeth Tudor had never taken Leicester or Essex to
her bed. Because if she had done she too, being
but human, would then have owned a master.

Men did change so queerly, thought Penelope, beginning
to roll a sheet of paper into her machine ; and the
change came about so gradually that there was no
particular moment when it was feasible to say, " so
far and no farther " ; the balance swung so gently
that it was not until one scale bumped heavily that

you realised that there had been a disturbance at all;
and it was all done so genially.

She wasted another few minutes in thinking about
the subtle processes which had changed Terry from a
servant to a master, from a rather wistful love-sick boy
into a genially arrogant man. But there was no regret
and no self-pity in her meditations. She had enjoyed
the change as much as anybody, had actually engineered
its initial stages and now she was happily married, in
love with her husband and back at her work. What
more could she wish? Deliberately she selected the
opening words for her novel and began to pound away
at the typewriter.

She worked until four o'clock in the afternoon,
enjoying the flow of fresh inspiration, and ceasing only
from sheer physical weariness. Florrie, the maid installed
after the re-opening of the Dower House, who had never
seen Miss Shadow in a working mood, was a little surprised
and not very pleased at being asked at lunch-time for
a plate of sandwiches and a pot of tea in the study.
As she explained to Agnes, her partner in the work
which had once been Terry's, it would have been different
if the mistress had thought to ask for what she wanted
before lunch, which the master had ordered, had been
cooked and set in the dining room. Agnes, who did
not share Florrie's infatuation for Terry, grunted and
muttered to herself, " It's *her* house when all's said
and done." Agnes was a great consumer of literature,
and although Penelope Shadow was outside her humble
range she had a secret sneaking respect for " a writing
lady." She had been quite excited all morning by the
tapping that could be heard in the study. Agnes also
satisfied her starved dramatic instinct by vast draughts
of village gossip which Florrie, as a superior person,
despised and she had listened to innumerable and not

unembellished accounts of the marriage between her
master and mistress. Florrie might think that anyone
was lucky to get Terry for a husband, but Agnes was
inclined to reckon that the luck was on the other side.

At four o'clock Penelope, feeling stiff and sticky,
took a bath, and while she was soaking in the fragrant
hot water she had an idea. Following it, she dressed
carefully in a new pink two-piece which she had not
worn since her return to Canbury, and then, entirely
unconscious of offended Florrie over the lunch, went
down to the kitchen.

"We shan't be in to dinner," she said. "I shall
go to Strebworth and meet the train and then Mr.
Munce and I will eat at the hotel." The words "master"
and "mistress" never fell from Penelope's inhibited
tongue, she thought them hurtful, terribly class-conscious.

"But the master's got the car," said Florrie, whose
dislike for sudden changes of plan extended even to
disliking an evening of unpremeditated freedom. Agnes,
who had already prepared the vegatables, knew no such
resentment. It was in keeping that "writing ladies"
should be sudden and unpredictable.

"I shall go in by bus," said Penelope.

Bumping along the dusty sun-and-shade-checkered
road in that vehicle Penelope felt pleased with her
plan. Terry would be very much surprised to see her
at the station, he would not have to wait so long for
his meal, and it would be, in a mild way, an evening
out. She realised, as the bus jogged into the town,
that as soon as she left her imaginary company of Tudor
people she had missed Terry very much. It had been
pleasant to have the day to herself, but it would be
nice to see him again.

The train was due at half-past seven. At fifteen
minutes past the hour Penelope, having retrieved the

car from the parking place, drove to the station entrance,
took up a prominent position facing the barrier and
lighted a cigarette.

As the train came in she cast a hasty glance at the
mirror and saw with satisfaction that her hair was in
order, her powder properly applied and that the pink
two-piece was kind and becoming. She was still inclined
to be careless and slap-dash about her appearance, but
she had been, for two years now, activated by a genuine
desire to look as young and as pleasing as possible, so
that Terry might think well of her and the difference
in their ages not be too apparent.

People began to stream out of the station and soon
she saw the figure for which she was looking. He was
not alone. There was a man with him, and two girls.
They were all what Penelope instantly identified as
" cheap smart " ; but while the man and one of the
girls looked ordinary, the kind of couple found in its
thousands in London, at the races, and at the seaside,
the other girl was really rather arresting. She was as
tall as Terry, that is, slightly above average for a woman ;
she had a full bust, rather obtrusive hips, and a very
small waist. Her checked suit of black and white fitted
her opulent figure so closely that it seemed to be painted
on her. She wore no hat and her long black hair fitted
her head like a wig of painted wood. The fringe curled
in just above her blackly marked eyebrows, the rest of
it turned in and rested upon her shoulders. Her mouth,
her jumper and her finger-nails were all dark cherry
red. Even in the moment while Penelope studied the
four of them she saw several men turn for a stealthy
second glance at the girl. She was very decorative,
and in a way spectacular.

The four came to the entry of the station, laughing
and talking. Then Terry separated himself, beginning

to move towards the place where he expected to find the car, leaving the three standing together in a little group, waiting. When he was three or four paces away the tall girl ran after him and took his arm, asking him something. Penelope saw him glance at his watch, lift one shoulder in a shrug and then answer her, affirmatively, nodding as he spoke. The girl held his arm for another second and then released it ; she walked back slowly towards her friends.

Penelope put her finger to the horn and pressed out a series of little sharp hoots. Terry spun round, saw the car and, altering his direction, sauntered towards her. His face, thrust in at the open window was a little redder than usual, his eyes rather furtive ; but his manner was normal.

" Hullo," he said. " Is anything the matter ? "

" No. I thought it'd be nice if I met you and we ate in town."

" I think it's nice too," he said, grinning. " Only," he shot a glance over his shoulder at the three waiting figures, " I'd kind of promised those folks a lift home. D'you mind if I just tell them it's off ? "

" We can go home . . . if it's going to cause much inconvenience."

" Lord, no. They weren't counting on me until a few minutes ago when I ran into them at the top of the steps. They'll manage. I shan't be a minute."

He ran across and seemed to be speaking hastily. The man of the trio looked about, and seeing an empty taxi waved his hand and called and began to run. The tall girl looked as though she were starting an argument, but the other caught her by the hand and pulled her along after the man. Terry ran back to the car.

Penelope moved out of the driving seat. " You can drive," she said. " Who were they ? "

" Cliff Axten, from the ' Shepherd and Dog.' You
know, the local. The tall one's his sister and the other
is his girl friend. They'd been to Newmarket, too."

" I see. Well, and did you have a good day ? "

" Oh, not bad," he replied, off-handedly. " I came
out about all square on the day."

She knew by that that he had lost money. Somewhere
at the back of his mind was the idea that she disapproved
of backing horses, probably because she never did so
herself and showed only perfunctory interest in racing
as a whole. And coupled with this idea was another,
that her disapproval would increase if he admitted
losing money. It made her a little sad, because it
showed a lack of confidence ; seemed in some way
to emphasise the difference in their ages, making her
seem like a parent, or a disapproving elder of some kind.

Tonight was not the first time it had happened ;
but tonight, thinking of it, as Terry drove to the hotel
and parked the car, she connected his disingenuous
answer about the racing with his unsolicited remark
about the Axtens, " I ran into them at the top of the
steps." She had an instinctive feeling that that was
not true either. The group had had the air of four
people who had been together longer than it would
take to descend the station steps.

God, she thought with impatient disgust, I'm getting
to *be* a suspicious, disapproving elder, thinking things
like that about Terry. She looked at him dotingly as
he took his place opposite her at the little table. No
other woman in the room had so handsome and gay
a companion ; no other woman in the world, she was
certain, had a husband so kind and thoughtful. What
if he had lost money today ? What if he had spent
his time with those rather shady-looking people. God
knew his life was dull enough, and his position as regards

friends very difficult. She had seriously thought of
selling the Dower House and living elsewhere after her
marriage, but Terry himself had dissuaded her, brushing
away her diffidently-spoken little reasons for a removal
with laughter and gay words. " I don't mind what
people say. . . ." " I like the Dower House ; I'm
marrying you merely to stay in it . . ." and things of
that kind, until she felt that to press the point was
to underline the potential awkwardness of the situation,
and with her usual method of retreating from difficulties
she had compromised by making the visits to Europe
and America, giving gossip time to die down. And
she had resolved sternly upon her return that if the
few people who were her friends resented visiting the
house where the former houseboy was now master, they
could stay away. She had fluffed up rather like a fiery
little kitten at the very thought.

Outwardly the whole thing had passed off very well.
The Willises were still friendly, so was Oliver Watling,
and Babs and Arthur Morrison ; but even so Terry
lacked men friends, young men of his own age and
tastes. And if Cliff Axten of " the local " supplied a
need, well, she had known from the first that Terry's
early life had not been calculated to breed lordly tastes.

Even remembering the prettiness of the Axten girl,
and the way she had held Terry's arm shouldn't make
her jealous. It should not.

She leaned across the table.

" On the way home shall we call at Marsdon's and
ask about the farm ? "

Terry's face lighted. " So you have thought about
it again ? I thought perhaps you'd given up the idea."

" No, I had honestly forgotten it. You should have
mentioned it again, darling. You know how I forget
things."

"I didn't like to. It's a hell of a lot of money. But I would slave at it, and pay you back." His face had a thin, eager expression, nearly akin to hunger, and Penelope remembered that the Irish were reckoned the most land-crazy race on the earth.

"You shall have it—if it's really for sale. And please don't say 'pay you back.' I thought we'd beaten that to death."

"It's a cat with ninety-nine lives when you're placed as we are," he said, quite serious for once. "That's why I'd like . . . well, I'd like to try it."

Marsdon owned a farm in Canbury and there were rumours that it was for sale. Terry had carried the rumour into the Dower House and suggested, half jokingly, that Penelope should buy it and let him work it. Until this moment she had treated the idea with little real seriousness, for during the past two years Terry had made repeated suggestions for, as he termed it, "regaining his independence." He had proposed setting up a market garden in the grounds of the Dower House; turning the house into a hotel; taking shares in a garage in Strebworth; establishing a discreet gambling and night club in the same town. The first and second schemes had met with little enthusiasm from Penelope, though Terry had promised that the vegetables should not spoil her view nor the guests intrude upon her privacy. From the fourth scheme she had shrunk in horror, seeing, in her imagination, the screaming headlines which would one day be the inevitable result; the third of the ideas had gained her interest, but by that time Terry had changed his mind and Penelope had forborne to re-open the question, fearing that it might look as though she were anxious for him to go to work. Actually that was the last thing she wanted; she enjoyed his company and his full attention ; she considered that he more than earned his spending money by standing between her and the household cares ; and, although she hated to admit it even to herself, she had, the moment he made any proposal for stepping out into the world, a sneaking feeling of jealousy. Almost any occupation would bring him into contact with other women who could not help—it seemed to her infatuated mind—but succumb to his charms.

But tonight, so shortly after finding him in Miss Axten's company, she had begun to think very seriously about Marsdon's farm. It would have the double advantage of keeping him at home and of keeping him out of mischief. So she said, " On the way home shall we call at Marsdon's ? " And Terry, all unknowing, had June Axten to thank for the move which set him up in business on his own at last.

In the course of a year the farm, which had provided its former owner with a comfortable retirement, lost a great deal of money. Penelope made the transfers from her own account to that of the farm with admirable fortitude, for the novel about the woman pirate had repeated " Mexican Flower's " success and she was able to indulge her whims. But young Oliver Watling, who had always helped her with her Income Tax, took a different view of the matter.

Over retaining Oliver's services Penelope had shown one of her stubborn streaks ; she had even, under its influence, said words which could only be regarded as unkind. For, quite soon after their marriage Terry had offered to take over the business of filling in Penelope's returns and checking her demand forms. Indeed he urged that that was his rightful duty, since now, in the eyes of the law, he was responsible, not only for her debts but for her Income Tax. Penelope had laughed at that ; but investigation had proved it to be true, incredible as it sounded. Nevertheless she stuck, with the patient repetitiveness of a child to her first statement, that Oliver must carry on. When every other argument had failed she had said,

"But Terry he *knows* about it. You've never had any experience with Income Tax."

It was a fact ; but she was appalled to hear herself put it into words, and glanced at him quickly, prepared to see his face darken. But after a second's hesitation he grinned and said, "That's true." And Oliver Watling continued in office.

When Terry had been running the farm for a year, and the assessment form, together with copies of the accounts had been sent to Oliver to cope with, that young man, with a serious expression on his face, called to see Penelope in the middle of an afternoon.

"I want to talk to you," he said.

"About the taxes ? " He nodded and drew a sheaf of papers out of his pocket.

"Were these cooked ? " he asked with brutal frankness.

"Cooked ? You mean faked ? Oh no, Oliver. Let me remember ; oh yes. I did have a new typewriter, but I needed it, and you can see it if you like. It's grey, the old one was black, you remember I expect. And I spent so much on paper and postage. I shouldn't think anyone could question that. I should think my expenses come to less than anybody's—anybody making the same amount I mean."

"Nobody would deny that," he said, looking at her for a moment with the respect which even nice people find hard to deny to the successful. "It wasn't about that side that I called. Have you forgotten the farm ? "

Penelope had forgotten it.

"Oh yes . . . the farm. Yes, that has been awfully expensive. But . . . it'll improve in time, you know. Perhaps Terry doesn't really know much about it yet. But he's learning all the time, isn't he? Don't worry about that, Oliver. Just take the bad with the good—I did quite well this year, you know—it'll be all right."

His look of respect faded, giving way to his more usual " you dear, silly little woman " expression.

"But according to this Terry seems to have lost nine hundred and eighty pounds, Penelope. In a year! That's an awful lot of money. Don't you see, it means that the farm is a dead loss, a burden. Why, the average young fellow, on his own, you know, would very soon be bankrupt at that rate."

"Not bankrupt, with a farm of his own, surely, Oliver. There's such a thing as a mortgage, you know." She was delighted at this startling evidence of her own acumen. Oliver, after another look, decided to abandon the conversation.

"What I really came for," he said, "was to ask you . . . I mean to tell you, that I shall have to talk to Terry. I can't just let this go in. If I didn't question it the Income Tax people would. You see, it looks rather as though you were deliberately taking the good with the bad and running the farm to avoid tax. Do you see that ? "

"Could one do that? Because it is a fact. I'm good ; the farm is bad. They'll take that into account won't they? I mean Terry and I count as one person for taxing don't we ? Yes, I'm sure I was told that."

"I'll talk to Terry about it," Oliver repeated. "I wonder what made him think he could run a farm anyway ?"

"Well, he can," Penelope said defensively. "He has fields full of things. Lovely they looked, wheat and

barley and sugar beet . . . oh, and some beans that
smelt heavenly. And Oliver . . . if you talk to him
you're not to make him miserable. Don't ask *him*
what you just asked me, about what made him think
he could. He can. Truly. It's only that we need
time."

And sense, Oliver added to himself. Aloud he said,
" Will Terry be at the farm now ? "

" Oh yes. He works awfully hard, you know.
Sometimes he doesn't come in until dark. . . ." Dimly,
in the very back of her mind, she became aware that
she was defending Terry, and thereby admitting that
he was, in some way, at fault. " Everybody has bad
years sometimes," she said, irrelevantly.

" Well, maybe a little talk will help matters. And
Penelope . . . if there's anything you or Terry don't
really understand about farming, you could ask me.
I nearly took it up myself. My father farms, you
know."

" Thank you, Oliver. That's very sweet of you.
You go along and talk to Terry and see if you can find
where the money's gone to."

She smiled him away and went back to work, feeling
snug and comfortable. It was very nice of Oliver to
take her losses so seriously, and now that he was interested
he would probably give Terry lots of helpful tips. In
two minutes she had forgotten all about the farm.

But Oliver, throwing himself into his rather rackety
car was in a disgruntled mood. He had never been
fond of Terry ; and he knew that this lack of fondness
had hardened into a more definite feeling when Penelope
had announced that she was marrying her houseboy.
Probably that news was a greater shock to Oliver than
to any other of Penelope's small circle of friends ; for
it had shown him, in one blinding flash, exactly how

fond of her he was, and what an unrealistic attitude he had been adopting towards her. He had never, never in his wildest moment dreamed of marrying her himself; it wasn't a feasible idea at all; to him Penelope had always seemed so different from any other woman, not quite an earthly being at all. It was absurd to imagine her marrying anyone. As for marrying Terry Munce, with his so obvious good looks; his too easy charm, his over-abundant self-confidence and his very dubious origins . . . it was horrible, Oliver thought.

And now he was certain that the position held elements of disaster as well. Nine hundred and eighty pounds down on a year's work; and that in a good year. And Penelope so vague; so loyal. Why, the chap could ruin her at that rate in a very short time.

The house at Yew Tree Farm was unoccupied. Terry had made some attempts to let it, but it was unmodernised and rather far off the road. So on this afternoon it stood empty and unfurnished, save for one room at the back of the house, looking across the yard, which Terry had fitted as an office. From the window he had evidently seen Oliver's car arrive, and now he came to the back door of the house and, with the pleasant diffidence of manner which he always assumed to those in whom he sensed distrust, invited the lawyer inside. He was proud of his office with its orderly files of paper, its shelf of agricultural and veterinary literature, its telephone and comfortable chair. He had no means of knowing that to Oliver Watling, whose father had run three successful farms and had kept his papers stuck in the frame of the overmantel mirror and had done his writing on the corner of the diningroom table, the office was an offence, a piece of playacting matched by Terry's chestnut corduroy breeches and open-necked shirt and polished brown boots. The boots were much too clean . . . and Terry shouldn't be lounging in an office at this time of the afternoon. Play-boy parasite, Oliver thought, as he stated his business with unnecessary brusqueness. Terry, offering cigarettes, offering whisky, and having both offers refused, reached at last, with smothered reluctance, for his account books. Very soon he was ardently regretting that Penelope had been so obstinate about retaining Oliver's services. It was the first time in his life that he had come up against a really trained mind. It wasn't a pleasant experience.

Two days later, after some daylight hours spent in pursuing inquiries, and some hours of darkness spent in wondering whether this were a matter which could tactfully be brought to Penelope's attention, Oliver called again at the Dower House and accepted Penelope's invitation to tea in the garden. Seated there in the cool shadow of the beech tree, looking at the beds full of second-crop roses and the lavender hedges turning mistily blue, he almost changed his mind again, thinking —I've given that young man a good fright and to tell her about it is likely to make mischief between husband and wife ; and it's just possible that she does know about it. . . .

Then Penelope said with her most anxious-kitten expression,

" How did you get on the other afternoon, Oliver ? Terry seemed rather gloomy when he came home. I didn't like to bother him with questions."

" I found what was wrong," Oliver said in a rather flat voice.

" Didn't I know the worst ? " she asked, frightened by his tone. " Had we lost more than that ? "

" The farm needn't cause you much anxiety. Penelope, tell me, how much are you interested in racing ? "

" Not a bit," she said happily, relieved by his words about the farm. " I don't care for it and I think betting is silly. But Terry adores it. And after all, Oliver, he must have *some* fun."

Oliver's last scruple vanished in a flash of jealousy. *He* had never had much fun. Even when he was attending his Grammar School he had done chores on the farm night and morning and in the holidays, and later, spurred on by the necessity of making a success of the profession he had adopted against his father's wishes, he had worked harder than ordinary. The thought of Terry, lounging in that office with cigarettes and whisky, when he should be out working, Terry having fun at the expense of this funny, dear little simpleton, transformed him from a tactful professional man into a crudely jealous human being.

" Then did you know that you owned a racehorse, or part of one ? " he asked.

" Don't be silly, Oliver. How could I own part of a horse ? "

" Six hundred pounds of that deficit, Penelope, is accounted for by the fact that Terry, a local publican named Cliff Axten, and an ex-jockey named Tommy Stebbing, between them bought a racehorse called Nerissa. She cost twelve hundred pounds, of which Terry found six and the others between them the remainder. Quite a large proportion of the remaining three hundred and eighty pounds is accounted for by the fact that, having purchased the animal, Axten and Stebbing were spent out and Terry has been meeting the trainer's bills. Racehorses are expensive pets."

There was venom in the last sentence, and as it was spoken Oliver cast at Penelope a searching, yet careful

glance. Had he shocked her too much, too suddenly?
But Penelope was not looking at all shocked. Her
expression, if anything, was conscience-stricken.

"D'you know," she said in a low voice, "I believe
that Terry *did* mention that horse to me. And I clean
forgot, as usual. As soon as you said the name, Nerissa,
it sounded familiar." She narrowed her eyes and then
blinked, trying to gauge the expression on Oliver's face.
So that's the way you stand up for him, that young
man was thinking, with a curious mixture of fury and
admiration.

"Whether you forgot it or not is not the really
important point," he said in a more professional voice.
"As I pointed out to Terry yesterday afternoon, a
racehorse is not essential to the running of a farm and
cannot be considered an allowable expense. To class
it amongst the farm horses as a purchase, and to offer
its price and the expense of its keep as proof that the
farm has run at a loss during the current year, is
definitely illegal. You're lucky, both of you, that I
made the discovery and had time to put the matter
right."

"Yes," said Penelope, meekly. "We are very lucky.
It shan't happen again. We'll learn."

For some reason the repetition of the first person
plural annoyed Oliver Watling excessively.

"Look here," he said, "it's none of my business,
but if I were you I should come to some more definite
arrangement about that farm and about Terry's spending.
The loss on the farm this year was negligible, even
counting the fact that it was its first year and the
most expensive one. Next year, with care and sense,
it should pay its way. Why don't you let me work
out what I think is a suitable sum and place it in the
farm's account, and then keep that quite separate?

What you let Terry spend on his sport, in addition to what he makes by working the place properly, is entirely your affair, of course ; but if you don't keep handing out sums, as you have been doing, it'll be an incentive to him to attend to his business. Do you see that ? Apart from everything else, Penelope, he's a young man, and not a very settled or experienced young man. You're doing him a moral wrong if you lead him to imagine that finance is something he can juggle with. Putting down a tenth-rate racehorse as expenses alongside that beautiful Shire mare ! Do you see what I mean ? "

'" Yes," said Penelope, with unusual firmness, " I do indeed. Elsie . . . that was my sister, you know . . . always gave the children pocket-money when they were small and then spending-money later on, and made them pay for their own pictures and for some of their clothes. She said it taught them responsibility. That's what you mean, don't you? I will do that, Oliver. I'll tell Terry that he must *make* the farm pay."

So Oliver Watling drove away from the Dower House thinking, but without the satisfaction that he had expected, that he had put a spoke in a young wastrel's wheel. And neither he nor Penelope could have guessed that on that day, by that very reasonable proposal, he had forged another link in the queer chain of destiny which had begun when Penelope Shadow rang the bell of the Plantation Guest House.

" But I tell you, she's gone mean on me now," Terry said, disengaging himself from June's arms and sitting back in the corner of the car. " Honest, honey, I'd let you have it if I could, but I just haven't got it. That damned Watling fellow worked out the wages and the expenses, cutting them to the bare bone and I can't draw another penny."

"You had a good enough allowance before you had Yew Tree. What's happened to that?" asked June, with the uninhibited frankness of the constitutionally coarse-grained.

"Every penny goes to that shark who is training Nerissa. And, honey, you do see, don't you, that I must hang on to *her*. It's our only chance of making some really big money and buying that pub for ourselves."

The focus of June Axten's attention shifted.

"You are really sure that she'd divorce you? Gosh, I can't think any woman would. Not really. No matter what you did?"

"I've told you a thousand times, if she didn't, I'd divorce her. Or at any rate I'd threaten to. She's crackers, honey. Raving crackers. I'd say that I was working on those lines. She wouldn't like it, and it wouldn't do her any good with what she calls her public. Why, d'you know, she daren't stay in that house a minute alone, after dark. Says the furniture moves about and the pictures sneer at her. She's mad and she knows it. I've only to say that I'll divorce her to save my own reason—not that that is grounds, mind, but she wouldn't know that, she doesn't know anything—and she'll divorce me quick enough."

"And you'll do it as soon as Nerissa has won The Thousand Guineas."

"The Thousand Guineas. And everything I can raise to back her. That's why, honey . . . you see, I could sell something off the farm and give you the money tomorrow. But I'm saving all I can to sell just before the race. Every penny I can raise on this muckheap is going to be used to back Nerissa."

"O.K. Then I'll go back and try to dress bitches' hair patiently."

"In Strebworth," Terry stipulated.

"Nerts to that. London. I ask you, Terry darling, would anybody in Strebworth know whether their few rotten hairs were properly done or not? I'll go back to London for eight months."

Terry's face darkened with the expression Penelope knew and dreaded.

"I'll not have you going back to London," he said. "You get a job in Strebworth."

June Axten's face hardened. "Honest, Terry, I can't. I did try. There isn't a job to be had. What I said about their few rotten hairs was sour grapes. I went all round yesterday, hoping to get a job so's I wouldn't have to bother you for money again. See, darling? It's London or nothing for yours truly." She gulped a little and added, "'Twon't be for long."

"It isn't going to be for any time. I'll get you some money. You stay right here. What'd I do without you?"

"But Terry, Angela won't have me home once they're married. She as good as told me so. And they're marrying on the fifth of September."

"That's nonsense. Angela was a pal."

"She *was*. Till that night at the station. Then she looked at *her* and began asking me about her and went off to the library next day and got out some bloody book called something flower—some jawcracky name or other. Anyway it made Angela howl like a wolf, and after that she . . . well . . . she just didn't like us going about together any more. Angela's like that. All sentimental. She's always putting pennies in boxes for Animal Societies or kids or starving foreigners. There won't be a place for me at the old ' Shepherd and Dog ' once Cliff gets himself hitched. That's a fact, Terry, not a joke."

"I've got an idea," said Terry, whose fertile brain had been burgeoning under this unpromising shower. "Why don't you come and live in *this* house?" He

jerked his head in the direction of Yew Tree Farm, just
visible from the tree-shaded spot where the car was
parked. " I'll bet you what you like that if I said Cliff
didn't want you down home when he married, and that
you were a fan . . . that's what they call people like
Angela . . . of *hers*, she'd beg you to live in it rent free.
And living needn't cost you anything. I could arrange
that, I order everything for the Dower House ; and I
could let you have milk and . . . and lots of things.
Darling, do do that. It's only for eight months. And
I could see you every day. It'd . . . it'd be as good as
being married almost."

" I'll think about it," said June, non-committally.
" What about the evenings, though ? Winter coming
on and all. It'll be a dull life."

" Not it," he said, with the confidence which formed
so large a part of his charm. " I'll be here. The cows'll
calve and the pigs'll pig and the horses'll all have families.
I'll be here most every night. She's got two people in
the house so she won't be scared, and if she's not scared
she'll hardly notice. Look, honey, if you'll do it I'll put
something in the market on Wednesday and give you
the dough for the furniture. . . ."

" Oh, I can get a few sticks from the pub. Some of
it was for me anyway. All the same, you sell something.
I can use some cash, Terry."

" That is where we came in," said Terry, taking her
in his arms again.

A little prick of jealousy made itself felt in Penelope's
mind when Terry mentioned letting the Yew Tree House
to June Axten. Disliking the idea that she was jealous
because June had such black hair, such an opulent figure
and such red finger-nails, and because she had run after
Terry and put her hand on his arm, Penelope allowed her

feeling to take the form of an unprecedentedly-sustained argument.

" What does a girl mean, wanting to live in such an out-of-the-way place all by herself, Terry ? "

" Well, she's been on the verge of a mental breakdown for some time now, darling. Between you and me, Cliff getting married upset her a lot. They're twins, you know, extremely devoted. And now Angela, that's Cliff's wife, won't have June in the house. June isn't as worldly as she looks ; the country means a lot to her. And, by the way, she's a great fan of yours. She said " Mexican Flower " made her howl like a . . . howl like anything."

" Can she pay the rent ? " asked Penelope, knowing that the last statement had weakened her defences, but determined to ignore the breach.

" Oh surely. Old Axten left quite a bit. Twenty pounds a year won't hurt her."

Penelope suppressed a desire to say, " You know a great deal about her," and said instead, " It's a good solid old house, I'd rather think of having a proper family in it . . . a man who could work on the farm or somebody like that."

" The farm hands all have cottages. And honestly, darling, nobody very solid would want it. It's miles off the road and a long way from a school. And terribly unmodernised, you know."

Penelope, thinking in terms of the psychology of fiction, thought, if there was . . . was any reason for the jealousy I'm feeling, he wouldn't want to bring her to my notice. He'd keep her out of sight. Oh I am *mean* to Terry ; just because I'm older and it's my money and I have a possessive nature. I mustn't be like that.

" I don't know quite what to say," she said, meaning that she did not know any further arguments against

taking Miss Axten as a tenant ; but Terry, misinterpreting,
said, a little crossly, "After all, Penelope, you wanted
me to make the farm self-supporting. One obvious way
is to let the house, anybody'd tell you that. And most
tenants would want God knows what in the way of
improvements. Then, when I offer you a country girl
who doesn't mind an oil lamp and . . . other incon-
veniences, you hum and ha as though I suggested something foolish."

"I know," said Penelope, capitulating. "Honestly,
I think it was largely because I couldn't face living like
that myself. If Miss Axten can bear it, good luck to her."

"That seems a rum thing to me," said Agnes, standing
in the pantry doorway, "but last Tuesday I would of
swore there was six pots of marmalade. One I opened
a-Thursday and now there's three. Seems I can't count
straight no more."

"If you ever could," said Florrie. "Almost every
time you look in there you have some such tale."

"Well, that sugar went, didn't it ? You know that
for a fact. And what about the better half of that ham ? "

"He came in hungry and cut at it. Who has a
better right ? "

"S'long as she don't think we gobble it up or make
off with it somehow."

"Is she likely to think anything about it ? How
often do she come in here ? " asked Florrie, dismissing
the subject.

Florrie judged rightly. The increase in the housekeeping bills consequent upon taking Miss Axten as a
tenant went entirely unnoticed. Penelope was far too
busy ; first with a group of personages in ruffs and
farthingales, and then with a mass of emotions which
were less manageable.

She stumbled upon evidence of Terry's intrigue by accident. June Axten had been installed at the Yew Tree Farm for just six months then, and almost everybody else in Canbury knew about it. Both Florrie and Agnes at the Dower House knew, for Agnes had heard about it from the village gossip and had relayed it to Florrie. That young lady, who was suffereing from a deep and secret passion for Terry, had, at first, under the spur of jealousy, known an impulse to tell Penelope. But a little consideration brought wiser counsel. Terry had at times shown himself not quite indifferent to her own charms, and since the affair with Miss Axten proved that he was extra-maritally inclined, and since such affairs seldom lasted long, Florrie's second reaction was one of bounding hopefulness. She might be next, one never knew. Anyway it was as well to keep one's mouth shut and not risk the scurvy treatment which was the traditional fate of bringers of bad tidings. Agnes would have died rather than tell Penelope, for her early devotion, fragilely based upon respect for Penelope's profession and a desire to be different from Florrie, had by this time reached solid dimensions. Penelope was always kind, and Agnes, who had not experienced much kindness in her life, appreciated it. And if Terry could " carry on " at the farm with another woman, and at the same time keep Penelope in blind happiness, Agnes was quite willing to aid and abet him by her silence.

Across the trees, at the new house, the Willises, too, had heard rumours. But Pamela Willis, a confirmed faddist, was at the moment busy practising a curious form of religion which insisted that its followers thought nothing but the best of their fellows. (There was a wave of this breed of thought abroad in the world at the time and several evil things flourished greatly because of it.) Pamela had many arguments with the more realistic Arthur, saying, " Just because she's young and pretty and lives there alone . . ." and " Nobody should be judged on circumstantial evidence . . ." and " So long as Penelope is happy not knowing, the *real* evil would be with the informer . . ." and other such things, more high-mindedly expressed. Arthur was by nature timid and hesitant ; he had a private conviction that, as Penelope's friend, it was his duty to tackle Terry, and once or twice, meeting him, had known an impulse to say, " Look here, what is all this I hear about you and some girl . . . ? But he had also a sneaking feeling that it was none of his business, and that Terry was capable of telling him so. And so he never mentioned the matter. Nobody else in the village was on sufficiently intimate terms with Penelope even to drop a hint ; the Morrisons and Oliver Watling lived at some distance and so were out of gossip's range. And there is no doubt at all that if any rumour had reached Penelope, it's very kinship with that unadmitted jealousy which had first driven her to buy the farm and then compelled her let June Axten live in the house, would have shocked her into the most vehement repudiation. As it was, nobody gossiped to her, or hinted ; and the situation into which she walked, all unprepared, was too obvious to admit of argument.

" February Fill-dyke " had lived up to its name that year. The month was eighteen days old and sixteen of those days had been teeming wet. Between Weeston and Southwyk the floods were out and numbers of cottagers had been obliged to leave their houses, climbing from the low upper windows into farm carts that were awash over their wheels. Canbury, on higher ground, had not suffered from flooding, but Agnes and Florrie, bored by being housebound, had started up a feud,

which, begun over some stupid triviality, had mounted
in intensity and in rowdiness until even Penelope,
submerged in the last chapters of the Tudor novel,
had not been able to ignore it. Stupid as she may
have been in overlooking its initial stages, she was
not, when faced with the final scene—Agnes tearfully
giving notice and Florrie exhibiting the place where a
plate flung by Agnes had found its mark—stupid at all.

" It's just being cooped up together for a fortnight
and not being able to get out," she said, quite calmly.
" I shan't *let* you leave, Agnes. But this afternoon
you must go and spend all the afternoon and evening
with your friends in the village—take some food with
you and make it a sort of picnic. And Florrie must
go to the pictures in Strebworth."

Their respective reactions were typical.

" That'll leave you alone in the house," said Agnes.

" The mud'd drag the shoes off me before I was to
the end of the lane, much less the bus-stop," said
Florrie.

" I shall go over to the New House," said Penelope.
" And Mr. Munce can drive you to the bus-stop, Florrie,
and you to the village, Agnes, when he goes back after
lunch. How's that ? "

Agnes, with a sniff which implied that she did not
mean to take a five-minute drive in Florrie's company,
announced that *she* had a pair of rubber boots and
would rather walk. Penelope, dismissing them both,
checked herself on the way to the telephone to ask
the Willises if she might visit them after tea, for it
occurred to her that Terry might, just for once, offer
to come in before dark and spend the evening with
her. He had been out so often lately. There was
always something to be seen to at the farm ; the animals
always seemed sick, the books perpetually in need of

attention. Often he was late for dinner; often he rang up and told her not to wait for him. And at the back of her mind, when she did think about it, which was not very often, Penelope sometimes wondered whether it were not partly her fault that he stayed in the house so little. She was writing so hard, and was so absorbed in her work that probably Terry found Miller, the stockman, and a sick cow better company. Subconsciously she had fastened on Miller, a wizened little man with heavy moustaches and a genius for veterinary work, as a chaperon for Terry and Miss Axten. Not that he was always needed. For Miss Axten was seldom alone in the farmhouse. She seemed very popular with her friends and relatives. Uncles and aunts and cousins were always staying with her, and when they failed there were friends from London and Norwich, from Ipswich and Colchester. If Penelope had even allowed her suspicions to be aroused she might have thought that though Terry was often ostentatiously ignorant of Miss Axten's affairs he never failed to catalogue her visitors. But Penelope was an artist, and she was busy. And Terry was unfailingly nice to her, indefatigable in attentions when he was at home, not a bit like she would have drawn an erring husband ; so very often for long stretches of time she forgot Miss Axten's very existence.

Actually, during this wet period, she had remembered that the farm had a tenant and had said once, " Miss Axten could surely make you a hot drink, Terry, when you come in wet." And Terry had said, almost ruefully, " She would, no doubt ; but she's away at the moment. Gone on a visit I believe."

So, on this mid-February day, disappointed in her hope that Terry would suggest an early return, Penelope had seen him off with a thermos flask of hot coffee and

a packet of sandwiches, because he would not be in
for dinner, and with Florrie, gaily and unsuitably
dressed, sitting by his side. Usually he rode a motor
cycle to the farm, but during this weather she had
persuaded him to take the car and was actually con-
templating the purchase of a second car for his use.

Soon after his departure Agnes strode off, her rubber
boot tops flopping against her legs, and in the suddenly
quiet house Penelope worked for an hour and a half
and then remembered about ringing the Willises.

" But of course, darling. We'll be only too pleased.
Walk! Good gracious, no. Arthur will pick you up
in the car at four. Of course it's no trouble. And
we'll have you all to ourselves till ten. Good. Goodbye,
darling."

Penelope had wanted to work until tea-time and to
leave the Dower House only when darkness threatened.
She had intended to walk through the woods to the
New House and was a little put out by Pamela's
arrangements for her welfare. But she washed, and
changed her dress, and made up her face and did her
hair and was ready when Arthur arrived punctually at
four o'clock.

Afterwards she remembered thinking that he looked
a little pale in the glowering afternoon light; but he
seemed cheerful enough and on the brief ride up to
the New House amused her by relating how the wet
spell had affected their household. The New House
parlourmaid and housemaid had behaved so identically
with Florrie and Agnes that Penelope had to laugh to
hear about it. Unfortunately Pamela, in her staunch
resolution to think the best of everyone, had hit on
no better idea than to tell the household what a perfect
character the parlourmaid was, and to give the parlourmaid a categorical account of the housemaid's virtues.

" So they both walked out the day before yesterday
and we're left with cookie. However, this morning
there were two letters, one from each of them, and
they'll each come back if the other doesn't ; so now
we're playing ' out you must go.' If Pamela asks you,
plump for the parlourmaid, will you, Penelope? Susie's
her name. She's my pick. Remember that. Susie
forever and let Winnie go."

Penelope promised ; privately preening herself on
having handled her own, exactly similar, crisis in so
much more sensible and profitable fashion.

There was no sign of domestic deficiency in the
New House, save Susie's absence from the dining-room ;
and without knowing it both Pamela and Arthur made
much of their guest, because they were secretly relieved to
have her by herself.   Terry, they admitted, was charming
enough, and, until the Axten affair, had seemed a very
harmless sort of fellow, but he was not of their class,
nor of their generation and any real intimacy was
impossible. So they made the most of Penelope's sole
company. At the same time Pamela, partly sticking
consistently to her role, and partly giving Terry the
honour due to Penelope's husband, was thoughtful
enough to say, at the end of the first course of the meal,

" I'll ask Cookie to keep the rest of this hot for Terry.
You said he'd be here at ten, didn't you ? "

" Yes. Ten punctually. That's very kind of you,
Pamela."

They were back in the drawing-room, drinking coffee
beside a cheerful log fire and commenting viciously
upon the rain, which could be heard again, after a
twenty-hour pause, lashing at the windows, when Arthur
Willis said suddenly, " Pam, I do feel odd . . .,"
dropped his coffee cup, which shattered upon the parquet
floor, and fell forward out of his chair.

Pamela, with more control than her devotion to cults would have led Penelope to expect, took charge of the situation. The two women lifted him on to the chesterfield, and Pamela, throwing a cushion aside, said,

" He has to lie flat. It's his heart, you know." She pulled open a little drawer in a table and took out a flat, round box. " Usually he has more warning and can swallow one of these and lie down. I'll get some brandy."

She spoke as though her husband were prone to such attacks and as though she were concerned, not unduly alarmed. But after the brandy had been administered and Arthur, restored to consciousness, had swallowed his tablet, Penelope saw her glance at the clock and sit down by his side, unostentatiously taking his hand in her lap and laying her finger on his pulse. The clock ticked ; and an expression of dread dawned on Pamela's face. After seven minutes had crawled by she said softly,

" Is it working ? Do you feel better, darling ? "

He shook his head, an almost imperceptible movement.

" Shall I call Doctor Carter ? "

" Please . . ." the breathy little word was scarcely audible.

" I'll do it," said Penelope.

" Strebworth two double two," said Pamela with sinister familiarity.

The telephone at the New House was set, with more artistry than convenience, inside an old sedan chair in the hall. In her hurry Penelope caught her forehead a stunning blow as she entered this amateur kiosk, and for a moment afterwards confused the ringing in her ears which resulted, with the re-assuring sound of activity at the Exchange. But after a moment she realised that the telephone was dead. She knew that

Pamela had an extension beside her bed, and her muddled mind suggested that it might be more responsive ; so, knocking her head again in the panel above the door and barking her ankle on the panel below it, she left the kiosk and dashed up the stairs. But, since the obstruction lay about midway between Canbury and Strebworth, where a huge tree, root-loosed by the floods and gale battered, had fallen and broken the line, the telephone by Pamela's bed was as dead as the one in the hall.

Only too sharply aware that Pamela would attribute the whole failure to her bungling, Penelope ran back into the drawing-room and gasped out that the telephone wouldn't work. By this time there was a faint blue shadow around Arthur Willis's mouth and nose, and the exterior calm of Pamela was obviously a mere cloak for mounting dread. At Penelope's words a feeling too desperate for mere irritation seized the mind of Arthur's wife . . . of all the people to have around in a crisis, she thought. But aloud she said, " Stay by Arthur, please, and I'll try." She vanished into the hall ; but in a moment she was back, defeat in her face.

" Something's wrong," she said, and Penelope could see that Pamela too knew moments of helplessness. It roused resource in her.

" Never mind," she said. " I'll take your car and go to the farm. The telephone there may be all right. If it isn't I'll get Terry to go to Strebworth. He drives awfully fast and Yew Tree is on the way. It won't waste a moment."

" Oh, bless you," said Pamela, dribbling a little more brandy through Arthur's lips. " Two double two, don't forget that. And go to the garage through the side door, it's raining."

In a surprisingly short time there came first the rattle

of the garage door and then the sound of a car, brusquely
started. Never again will I let even Arthur laugh at
her, Pamela Willis thought. Then it occurred to her
that Arthur might never laugh at anyone again. This
was not one of his usual attacks at all. She looked
at the clock and began to count minutes, thinking about
the possibility of the Yew Tree telephone working, or
remembering the numbers of times when she had seen
Terry Munce driving recklessly along the familiar road.

Almost every fixture inside the Willis car was in a
different position and of a different kind from those
in Penelope's own. It had an idiosyncracy in the
steering, too, pulling heavily to the left as though
weighted. And the rain was like a solid wall of water.
But Penelope, awkwardly grappling with the unfamiliar
wheel and driving the accelerator pedal into the floor-
boards, was, with her natural carelessness and long
sight, as good an emergency driver as Pamela Willis
could have found, and in the least time possible was
bumping along the bit of private road that served
Yew Tree as a farm drive, and after a series of jolts
and dives was at the main gate, where, in the light
of her headlamps, she could see her own car parked
under the shelter of a cart shed. Knowing Terry, it
occurred to her that there must be some reason why
he left the car outside the gate instead of driving into
the yard, for he never walked if he could help it ; and,
since the gate looked awkward, she stopped on the
far side of it and descended. Once through the gate
she knew why the car was parked on the far side of it,
for just within was a sticky quagmire into which her
feet sank, coming up again with a gluey sucking sound.
It went through her harassed mind that she was glad
she had left the car outside, so heavy a machine could
easily have bogged in this ; and she was glad too that

her shoes had straps, court shoes would have been torn from her feet. Then she was out of the bog and on to the cobbles, and holding her hands in front of her she groped her way to the back door. It was locked, and she thought with sharp despair, remembering that blue shadow on Arthur's face, that Terry was in some outbuilding or stable. She did not know her way about the farm : and in the downpour of rain she could see no light : hear no sound. The office window to the left of the door was dark when she fumbled her way to it and she thought, now I must drive on to Strebworth and coming here has really been a waste of time. She was actually making her way back to the car when a new thought struck her. Terry might not be there, but the telephone was, and if she could use it she would be saving precious moments after all. If June Axten had come back from her visit, or if there were a door or window open, it would be easy to use that telephone.

The brave thought had carried her around the corner and to the side of the house before her old terror of empty houses asserted itself. It came upon her more coldly than the rain which had plastered her hair flat, soaked her clothes and was running in icy streams down her stomach and legs. She was sick with terror, knowing that should the house reveal no trace of human habitation, it was her bounden duty to enter the place by any means that offered, fumble her way through the darkness of a strange house and reach that office. Weak thoughts about this being a waste of time, that it would be quicker to drive on to Strebworth, or to cut across and use the telephone from the Post Office in Canbury, occurred to her. But she was frightened even to think of such expedients. She was a coward . . . she always had been . . . but even cowards were compelled to be

brave when it was a matter of life and death. Crying
now from terror and vague self-pity she fought her
way along the side of the house. There seemed to be
a great many bushes growing thickly and closely to
the house wall. They stopped her and tore her face
and dress and frightened her more than ever . . . they
seemed conscious and malignant, and if this could happen
outside the house what might not the inside threaten?
Moaning a little, she struggled clear of a vast, sharp-
prickled rose bush, and as she rent her ruined dress out
of its clutches she saw, with the sweetest sense of relief
that she had ever known in all her life, that the window
about which the rose had once been trained to climb,
was faintly golden with light. Somebody was there.
She thrust her head forward and stared, instinctively
drawn to the light, to the thought of a human presence.

It was quite easy to see into the room, nothing but
some thin curtains, carelessly drawn, and the loose
strands of the tumbled rose bush shielded it from the
gaze of the outsider.

Within the room, lit by the light of a leaping fire
and the light of an oil-lamp with a pink shade, was a
scene that was theatrical in its setting, its meaning,
and its almost careful direction of detail. A curtain
rising and leaving an audience staring at such a scene
would convey a message there was no mistaking. The
soft lights, the divan by the fire, the seductive female
body hardly shrouded at all by the folds of the scarlet
negligé, the little table set with a bottle and some
glasses and some food, the male body, slightly ridiculous
because men do not look their best in déshabillé : all
so eloquent that its meaning could be gathered at a
glance, no more ambiguous than a shouted obscenity.
Penelope needed waste no time staring at it. Telling
herself stoutly that she was *still* relieved to find some-

one in the house, she lifted her hand and with her
knuckles and the face of the heavy signet ring that had
been Grandfather Shadow's, she beat sharply on the
window. And as soon as she had thus drawn attention
to herself she called Terry by name.

And it was still like being at a play, to see the two
figures leap up ; to see the terror and the look of guilt-
discovered on their faces ; to see the woman's hands
frantically drawing the negligé close, the man's doing
complicated things with buttons and sleeves. The
wronged wife's speech was, perhaps, a little out of
character. She said sharply, "Don't waste any time.
Let me in. I want to use the telephone."

Once inside she brushed them aside as though they
were really the mopping, mowing idiots that they felt
themselves. "Get a light, Terry, and show me the
office." And when that telephone, so hardly fought
for, proved useless as the other, she said, as calmly
as she might have said it had she found Terry working
in the office, "Then you'll have to fetch Doctor Carter,
Terry. Arthur Willis is very ill. Maybe dying." He
moved to the door, white-faced, obedient as a child,
and she called after him, "I shall go back to the New
House. Call for me there."

He ran out into the rain. Penelope stood for a
moment in the middle of the little office, her right hand
still resting on the telephone, her left hanging loose
at her side. She thought, of course, I've known for a
long time, really ; and, I must get back to Pamela.
She thought the two things alternatively for what seemed
a long time. Then a sound from the doorway made
her turn her head, and she saw June Axten just outside
in the passage. From chin to toe she was covered
now in cherry-coloured silk ; her hair was smooth and
solid-looking as ebony, her face composed. But there

was a nervous tremor in the cherry-tipped hand which lifted a cigarette to the smudged cherry-coloured mouth and lowered it again.

She said, and her voice, though slightly common was not unattractive, " I'm sorry you come on us like that. Terry was going to tell you about it and ask you to divorce him."

Penelope could think of nothing to say. There was a little tie belt of narrow velvet ribbon around the girl's waist, and above it her bosom swelled, rounded, firm, yet soft ; and below it there was the opulent curve of her hips. Suddenly Penelope remembered her first reading of the Song of Songs which is Solomon's. A cheap little floosy, perhaps, but very lovely ; a honey-pot of a girl, made for a man's undoing. She felt herself, all at once, brittle and old and tired ; nerves and bones too near the surface, rheumaticky, inky, queer.

" You're very beautiful," she said, speaking as though the sound of her own voice surprised her a little. Then she remembered that she must get back to Pamela, so, passing the astonished girl in the passage, she made her way to the door, plodded through the mud, got into the car and drove rapidly back to the New House.

Penelope, like a good many people of fragile appearance who suffer mildly from chronic ailments, had never known a real illness in her life, and the bout of pneumonia which followed her soaking on the night of Arthur Willis's death, frightened her badly.

She had got back to the New House, soaked to the skin, and suffering from a kind of shock which rendered her more than usually susceptible to chill ; and she had stayed in her wet clothes, helping Pamela in that last struggle to keep Arthur alive until the doctor arrived, and then comforting her under the first sharp

shock of bereavement. And when it was all over she
was feeling too ill and too tired to regard Terry as
anything save a kind friend to whom she could say,
" I feel so awful, Terry, you'll have to help me to bed."
It would have been difficult for an observer to credit
that this man, so deftly and gently putting his wife
to bed, carrying hot toddy, filling hot-water bottles,
stripping off mud-stiffened shoes and stockings, had,
three hours earlier, been taken in the very act of
adultery. And Penelope was dimly aware of the
incongruity in the situation ; but her mind was already
slipping into a fever-ridden country and almost her last
conscious thought was that Terry might be naughty
but he was also very kind, with a kindness for which
she was supremely grateful.

She was not frightened during the actual illness itself,
she was too sick for any feeling save that of pain ; but
afterwards, when she was on the way to convalescence,
she became convinced that she was going to die.
Nothing else, she thought, could account for her lassitude,
her despondency. Even the two poles of her simple
life—Terry and the book upon which she was working—
seemed unreal and unimportant. She would die and
Terry would marry that lovely girl ; and the book
would never be finished now. Neither of them had any
lot or part in this poor shell of Penelope Shadow which
lay on its bed, with the bones wearing through the
skin where the bed pressed, with its hair dry and lank,
its fingernails cracking and its vitality so spent that to
draw a breath seemed to demand an effort.

When Doctor Carter suggested to Terry that she
should be taken from her bed and moved to a chair
by the window, so that the March sunshine might cheer
her and the sight of the resurrecting garden take her
out of herself for a few minutes, Penelope cried and

clung to her bed and thought both the doctor and Terry
very heartless indeed.

And when at last, despite her protests, she was moved
to the window, the sight of the bulbs pricking through
the black soil of the borders, the faint presage of green
on the hawthorn hedge, the red buds of the elm trees,
moved her to further maudlin tears because she was
certain that she would never see the daffodils or the
tulips which would spring from those bulb-spears, nor
the hedge white with blossom, nor the elm trees like
full-sailed ships against the summer sky. And in this
mood she begged Terry to bring a pencil and paper
and jot down her last wishes.

He was much moved by this request, but hardly in
the way which Penelope, full of self-pity, had intended.
The *affaire Axten* had never yet been mentioned between
them ; and he wondered for a moment whether Penelope,
under the first pricking of returning life, were taking
this method of letting him know that he had forfeited
his interest in her estate. But she really looked so
pitiable and harmless that he could hardly credit her
with such spite. And anyhow, he thought, if she gets
me to write anything awkward I shall tear it up. So,
turning away to hide his discomposure, under pretext
of searching for a pencil, though he had one in his
pocket, he steadied himself, and with a gentle jeer at
her morbidity, sat down to make a note of her wishes.

" I have made a will," she began in a voice which
croaked, partly from weakness, partly from recent
tears. " Oliver made it soon after we were married.
I left everything to you, Terry. But there were a few
little things that I didn't like to bother him about,
and I knew you'd see to them for me. . . . I'd like Elsie
to have all my Grandmother Shadow's silver, you know
which that is. She isn't a Shadow, but she's the only

relative I have and she'd cherish it. Nobody else
would, it's so antiquated. And I'd like Mary to have
my furs. She's young and won't be able to afford
really nice ones for a long time. She could have my
emerald ring, too. I did buy that, because I always
wanted an emerald just to look at, for some reason.
I never wear it, but it's with my other things. Elsie
can have the rest of them, except this ring I always
wear; that was my grandfather's and I'd like Richard
to have it. And I'd like it, too, if you'd ask Pamela
Willis and Babs Morrison to choose something from
the house, just to remember me by. Oh, and Agnes
and Florrie should have something. Twenty pounds
each, perhaps. They've had a lot of work running up
and down. That's all. And I'd like to be buried in
Much Wrenny churchyard."

Her voice broke again in a luxury of self-pity.
Though why I should cry, she thought vaguely, I can't
understand; I certainly don't want to live, feeling
like this. Terry, who had been moving the pencil
obediently, and to whom only one sentence of her speech
had any significance at all—" I left everything to you "
—now put paper and pencil aside in an ecstasy of
relief, for if she had intended to alter her will at all
she would not have left these last requests in his charge,
and surely that must be taken as a sign that she had
forgiven him. He knelt down beside her and took her
hands, and after assuring her that she was not going to
die, suddenly hid his face in the rug that covered her
knees and with many flowery phrases and a great deal
of Celtic self-abasement, said that he was sorry about
his lapse with June Axten; it was nothing except
proof of his vile nature, it was nothing to do with his
love for Penelope; just madness, the sort of thing no
woman could understand. And if Penelope could find

it in her heart to forgive him, it should never happen
again.   They'd go away and she should have a holiday
which would restore her entirely and he would be her
devoted, contrite and ever loving husband until the end
of time.

And to that speech the strain of oddity in Penelope
responded. For that phrase, "the sort of thing no woman
could understand," had pricked her pride as an artist.
It was the duty, and the privilege of an artist to see
with eyes, feel with nerves, not her own.   And remembering her own reaction to the sight of June standing
like a lovely flower, ivory and scarlet and black, in
the dimness of the farmhouse passage, Penelope said,
in quite a new voice,

"But I *do* understand, Terry. I understood that
very evening. She is so beautiful. And so young."
The unspoken words, "I am neither" hung on the air.

Despite his great relief Terry was conscious of feeling
shocked.

"All the same," said Penelope, rousing herself a
little, "I'd rather she didn't live there any more."

"She's gone," he said.   "She's been gone three weeks."

He lifted his head and stared at Penelope, his vivid
blue eyes like those of a dog which has done the most
forbidden thing, but is very, very sorry and will never
even look in that direction again.   And she, remembering
how through the pains and the dreams and the torments
and the wandering in uncharted lands which she had
lately known the one constant thing had been Terry's
presence, Terry's kind reliable presence, felt a curious
sense of shame.   She asked gently,

"Were you telling me the truth, Terry, about not
loving her? You must tell me the honest-to-God
truth, now. Do you love her? Because if you do I
wouldn't stand between you."

" I told you," he said violently. " She's nothing to me. It was just a moment of madness ; and she after me every moment, never giving me any peace."

" Then I'll say, and I mean it, my dear, if ever you do find someone, beautiful and young, whom you do love, you must tell me. Until then we'll never mention the matter again."

This forward-looking was in bright contrast to the last-bequest mood in which the interview was started ; and by the time the pact had been sealed by a few vehement vows of love upon Terry's part, and some less wordy responses from Penelope, and the exchange of such careful clasps and kisses as were consistent with her state, she felt a great deal better and ate her lunch with appetite. And next day was glad to sit by the window and plan, first a walk in the garden, then a drive in the car, and then an onslaught upon the typewriter. Life at the Dower House resumed its normal course. The Yew Tree Farm house stood empty. Miss Axten, with fifty of Terry's ill-spared pounds in her red handbag, had gone to stay in Newmarket as a paying guest of the Stebbings with whom she could share the hopes and anticipations of Nerissa's triumph.

Spring blossomed all over England, and on a day of such rapidly alternating sunshine and shadow that it might be thought the clouds themselves were holding a race meeting, a crowd of gaily dressed people, most of them indifferent, a few, who had backed a long-odded outsider, with disappointment, and a few, connoisseurs of the sport, without surprise, watched a bright bay mare, with many showy points and an obvious lack of stamina, dash out to lead the field for a few dizzying seconds only to be passed, to fall behind and finish last but one.

" Well, that's that," said June Axten ; and though
there were tears in her brilliant eyes there was a note
of finality in her voice which added a spice of fear to
Terry's mood of black disappointment and rage.

" Let's get out of this," he said, looking at the crowd
as though he bore a personal grudge against each
individual in it.   " We've got to settle what to do."

" What to do," June echoed, hunching a shoulder
sceptically ; and then, after a glance at his face, she
turned meekly and followed him as he thrust a ruthless
way through the packed people. She had not seen
him in so black a mood before and mentally she braced
herself to carry off the interview which impended. He
would be difficult ; but she was going to be firm. She
had spent long enough messing about waiting on his
whims, waiting for his crack-brained schemes to come off.
Now he was broke, and she knew it, and she was through.

All the way back from the race-course into the town
she was thinking. It was all his fault, he had deceived
her from the start, making out to be so rich and grand,
when all the time he hadn't a penny of his own. In
her disappointment and suddenly awakened sense of
stark reality she forgot that for months she had been
living on Terry's allowance ; she forgot that they had
had good times together, and that he was better to
look at, more entertaining, and a more adept lover
than most of the men who came her way. She only
remembered that he had persuaded her to give up her
job, that he had deluded her for a long time with
promises of security and independence in the proprietor-
ship of a smart seaside hotel, and that he was a failure.
Also, nagging at the back of her splendidly insensitive
mind, was the memory of that cracked little woman's
behaviour on the night of the discovery. " You're
very beautiful," she had said, without rancour, almost

with wonder. Miss Axten, who had been living the
life of a predatory female since she was sixteen—she
was now twenty-four—had once or twice been faced
by wives, angry and suspicious ; she had never before
been caught so flagrantly, and she had never before
been called beautiful by any woman. The memory
stuck, like a burr, a very small, almost negligible burr,
but it played its part in her general mood of irritation
against Terry. Penelope had, for one tiny second, made
her feel ashamed ; and the experience was as unpleasant
as it was unusual.

So, when Terry had steered her into the rather shabby
little tea-shop, and, for the sake of its hospitality,
ordered tea and cakes, she looked ostentatiously at her
watch and said, " I mustn't stay too long. I must get
along to Tommy's place and pack my duds. I'd like
to catch the four-fifteen."

At the back of Terry's mind there was a strong desire
to put his head in his hands and cry. It was, perhaps,
the last weak impulse of his youth, which had, in the
last hour, met its death beneath four iron-clad hooves
that could not travel fast enough. But he knew that
the least sign of weakness now would lose him June ;
she would despise him for a poseur, for an optimistic
fool, and for a failure. And it was easy to fight back
the weak desire to shed tears of disappointment and
despair, because he was so angry. If malevolent
thoughts could have killed Cliff Axten and Tommy
Stebbing who had persuaded him into the purchase of
the damned horse, the man who had trained it, and
the owners and the trainers of every horse who had
outdistanced Nerissa, Newmarket would that day have
witnessed a holocaust. His feelings towards himself
were equally destructive, though of a different kind.
Everything in him which was happy-go-lucky and

optimistic had been stricken to death that afternoon, and he was left seeing himself as a stupid fool who had never really properly exploited his opportunities. He'd tried, with the farm and with Nerissa to *make* money, when all the while the money was there for the taking. He'd been soft with Penelope, letting her boss him about ; and he'd been soft with June, letting her frighten him into things. Well, now it was their turn. He glared across the innocent little table with its posy of flowers, its neatly mended checked cloth and cheap bright crockery, and said,

" You're not catching any train. You're coming back with me to Canbury."

June gave a laugh, a rather hollow laugh, but mocking enough to lend courage to her next words.

" Oh no, I'm not. I'm through, Terry, so I'm telling you quite frankly. I'm going back to London where there's a bit of life and a chance for a girl."

" You'll see what life and what chance you'll get if you do, my dear ! I'll dog every step you take and I'll smash in the mug of any man that looks at you twice."

" You wouldn't dare ! "

" Wouldn't I just ? "

She began to argue, thereby betraying her weakness.

" I don't owe you anything, Terry Munce. You had your money's worth. Didn't I live eight months down on that mouldy farm ? Might as well have been in a harem ? And fifty pounds at the end. Work that out and see what it comes to a week. And I've lost my job—and my home. I was always sure of a bed and my keep at Cliff's place before I took up with you. You let me go. If I'm ready to call it quits you should be."

" Well, I ain't," he said, reverting to the ungrammatical emphasis of his earlier days. " I'll tell you what

you're going to do. And you'll do it. You'll go back to
Cliff this afternoon when I drop you at the end of the
lane, and you'll tell him, and that snotty-faced little
she-parson he's married, that you're through with me
and want to stay there for a bit. Then I can see you
now and again while I look round." He saw the lack
of faith in her eyes. " You think that bloody mare was
my last throw, don't you ? Well, you're wrong. I've
got other irons in the fire, better ones. Only it'll take a
little time to hot them up. And you're not going to be
running round loose while they do it. See ? You may
think I'm poor and tied down ; but give me a little
time and I'll be rich and free as air and ready to marry
you . . . ." Heartened by these words, vague as they
were, he allowed his scowl to relax. He fixed her with
the blue stare which Penelope always found so under-
mining. " Come on, honey. Don't be a rat and desert
me just because I've taken a knock. You and me get
on fine, don't we ? Don't we ? You show a little faith,
and just make it up with Cliff and Angela, and wait.
It won't be long. You'll see."

" What are you going to do ? " she asked, interested
despite herself.

" You'll see." It was the most definite answer that
was in his power to give. For in truth he had no idea,
at that moment, how these plans for affluence and
freedom were to be put into action. He only knew that
Penelope had more money than she needed, and that he
did not intend to let June get away. Already his volatile
spirits were rising again. But the Terry who, with
June at his side, drove back to Canbury that afternoon,
was different from the one who had driven away from
the village that morning. In the morning, despite his
natural talent for deception, his mercenariness, his
heartlessness, he had been a romantic ; trusting in a

rosy future which would solve his problems, optimistic, bound still by a few scruples ; in the afternoon he was a realist, knowing that fate would do nothing for him, he must make things happen, he must throw his last scruples overboard.

From the day of Nerissa's defeat until the middle of June, was, despite the lovely weather and the beauty of the garden, less happy than any season Penelope had yet spent at the Dower House. It was at once very easy and very difficult to say what exactly was wrong. It was easy enough to see, and to admit to oneself, that the change lay in Terry ; but it was difficult to describe that change exactly. He was as kind as ever ; and as considerate to spare Penelope—now in the process of finishing the Elizabethan book—to carry the petty affairs of the household as well as see to the farm. In fact he was steadier and busier than he had ever been. But he no longer radiated cheerfulness. And yet, Penelope thought, when, as she often did, she thought about him, one could not call him glum. It was just that a kind of radiance, a sense of well-being and cheer which had hitherto always accompanied him, had gone. He seemed well, he spoke and acted cheerfully, but she was driven once more to think of Miss Slater and her "auras" ; the brilliance of Terry's aura was dimmed.

She tried, in her vague, kind, fumbling way, to draw out of him, by talk, some confidence which would give her the clue to the mystery. Was he, she asked, working too hard ? Couldn't he leave the farm for a while and take a holiday ? Was he tired of it, would he like to give it up ? She wouldn't mind a bit, she said. Was he worried about money ? That was the last thing she desired ; and if he were in any difficulty he must see Oliver and ask for what he wanted. There, of course, she was cowardly and made a mistake which was to cost her dearly. A fat cheque, or better still a blank one, might have postponed the evil day. But an interview with Oliver Watling was the last thing Terry wanted ; one was in the offing, certainly, and the thought kept him awake at night sometimes. And Penelope, who, rather belatedly, wanted her generosity to take the proper form, was consoled and deceived by his vehement assertions that everything was all right and that he did not need money.

In any case he would have found it difficult to tell her how much he wanted, and why. He had stripped the farm just before the race, as he had promised and planned to do, selling everything saleable and putting the money on Nerissa. And afterwards, shedding the queer scruple which had allowed him to rob Penelope indirectly but forbad direct stealing, he had twice forged her signature upon cheques made out to himself, and once, at the end of April, calmly paid into the farm account a pretty big royalty cheque made out to her and entrusted to him to pay in to her private account. The money thus obtained had enabled him to re-stock the farm to some extent, but it did nothing towards solving his real problem which was how to get enough money to set him free of Penelope and provide for himself and June.

So the days and weeks passed, and it was June, and Penelope worked away steadily, now and then thinking of Terry and coming to two very diverse conclusions. Terry was losing the first glow of youth, and sad as that might seem, it was in the natural order of things and, though it might be regretted, could not be helped. Or again, Terry had, in fact, loved that lovely girl more than he would admit, and was suffering secretly. When she thought this Penelope was seized with a form of schizophrenia. The artist in her was sorrowful and understanding ; she felt she had robbed him, taken his youth,

twisted his destiny : the woman fell victim of a sick
jealousy, far more bitter than that which she had known
at the moment of looking in through that window. A
lapse into lust did not strike at the basis of marriage as
a secret pining could do.

So through those few weeks Penelope was not very
happy either, except when she was banging away at her
story. And in the kitchen both Florrie and Agnes were
struggling with their problems too. Florrie was losing
hope. That painted Axten creature had gone away,
but she was back again, and people had seen her and
Terry together, the whole village was talking about it.
Florrie was going to spend the summer in this easy
pleasant place, but not another dull winter ; she was on
the look out for a job. Yet, since to an undeveloped
organism, a little lecherous desire unsatisfied, can be as
painful as a great unrequited love to a creature of greater
sensibility, she was suffering at the idea of going away
and never seeing Terry again. And Agnes was in the
painful process of changing what passed as her mind
over the matter of telling the mistress that she was being
deceived again. Once Agnes would have died rather
than breathe a hint of the matter ; and when Miss
Axten disappeared without the scandal having reached
the Dower House, she had been satisfied that she was
right. But now it was different. Right there in the
village the painted hussy was strutting about, and
although in actual fact the time when she and Terry had
been seen together the circumstances were accidental
enough, rumour was very busy ; and for the two people
who had actually seen them on that occasion, there were
twelve who saw, or thought they saw the pair under
stacks, behind hedges, and in the woods. It was, Agnes
reflected, making the mistress look like a fool ; and
though young Mrs. Axten down at the pub had been

overheard to say that if the affair hadn't been over she
wouldn't have had her sister-in-law in the house, you
never knew. Pub keepers and women who married them
couldn't be expected to have a very high standard either
of morals or truthfulness. On the other hand what could
Agnes say ? In what words did one break such news ?

Actually she broke it in her own words and without
any idea that Penelope was listening.

Penelope had been cutting roses, and because, years
ago, Grandmother Shadow had always put her flowers
into soft water, she had left the flowers on the table in
the hall, and, carrying the bowl, gone round to the little
scullery where there was a soft-water tap. She had
walked round the house and into the back door of the
scullery because it was more pleasant to walk along the
little lavender-bordered path in the sun than to go through
the kitchen and have Florrie and Agnes look up and
wonder what she wanted, or ask a question, or make a
complaint, or perhaps just think that she was a fuss-pot
to want soft water.

The window between scullery and kitchen was open,
for the day was warm, and the tap was just under the
window. The girls could have seen Penelope's head if
they had been looking that way, but Agnes was bent
over the stove and Florrie was lifting plates from the
dresser, loading a tray to carry into the dining room.
And there was nothing remarkable in the fact that they
were discussing Terry and Miss Axten, for they did that
every day ; it was almost the only subject upon which
they found themselves in agreement nowadays, though
their motives for interest in it and their real attitudes
towards it were poles apart.

"Well, I got a good mind to tell her myself," said
Agnes. She had been meaning for days to say that
and see how Florrie took it. Now she had said it.

" You thought different once."

" I know I did, but thass worse this time. Time she was at the farm that weren't so scandalous. Not so flaunting like. Whyn't you drop her a hint, Florrie? You'd put it better'n me."

" I should smile ! If she think you can keep a husband by hitting a typewriter all day and all night let her find out different for herself."

" But d'you know what they're saying now? Coo, I shouldn't really say this by rights. It was said to me very confidential. Mrs. Paine—you know, what worked here once—she say she shouldn't wonder if there's trouble a-brewing there. She reckon she's bigger in the belly than she should be."

" You don't say ! " said Florrie in a voice in which delight and horror were mingled.

" Thass what she said, honest. And owd women often hev an eye for such things. Coo, if thass right and there's a baby *she'd* hev to know. That painted thing is just the sort to bring an order shouldn't you think ? "

Florrie reached down a water jug from the shelf, and peered into a stone water jar of rather oriental appearance which stood under the dresser.

" Half a mo'," she said, meaning that she was relinquishing the interesting subject only temporarily. " You'll have to work that bloody well, Agnes. My saints ! If I was as fussy about water tasting fusty I'd have something done to them pipes."

There was a rattle as Agnes took up the pail. Penelope, making herself small, standing back in the shadow of the little scullery, watched, as though in a dream, the sturdy little figure step out into the sunshine of the paved backyard, throw up the well cover, hook on the pail and send it dipping into the cool depths below. It came up dripping silver, and Agnes, with her figure braced against its weight, trotted back into the kitchen. Penelope heard the smooth pouring of the water into the jar. It was strange, she thought, that the cool cleanliness of the well water should have become contaminated by its connection with this moment of sickness and misery. She had loved the well. Every summer the rather ancient water system of the Dower House seemed to feel the strain of supplying a twentieth-century household, and the water in the pipes tasted flat and stale. It was Terry—always Terry—who had suggested trying the well, and it had been opened and cleaned, yielding water so cool and so clear that there had been a sensuous pleasure in the thought of it as well as in the taste. Now it was fouled forever. Because Terry *was* in love with June Axten ; he had brought her back ; and all through the village people were talking just as Florrie and Agnes had been talking a moment ago—gloating over the details, pitying Terry's wife, or blaming her.

And with a sense of surprise at her own reaction, Penelope knew that it was the quality as well as the content of the gossip which was so horrible. It rolled everything in the mire. It made love filthy ; it soiled even an unborn baby. She was, at that moment, shocked and sickened to her very soul. She had always disliked being called a romantic novelist ; she had taken pride in calling a spade a spade, in admitting the existence of cruelty and baseness in the world. But never before in all her life had she come near anything like this. She remembered the beauty of the girl in the passage, and her own thoughts about youth calling to youth, loveliness to loveliness ; she had been willing to stand aside, to divorce Terry and let him go to his love—" golden girls and boys " they should be together. But he couldn't accept that, which would have been a comparatively easy sacrifice, because there would have been a cleanliness, a seemliness about it. No, he must say, " She's nothing to me " ; and then bring her back, so that people could roll their greasy tongues round words like " big belly " and " painted thing " and " bring an order." And at the same time they spoke of her work as though it were ridiculous, " hitting a typewriter all day and all night." Dear God, thought Penelope, this is intolerable.

She did not know that she was crying ; and she was surprised to find herself in the bathroom. She had no memory of entering the house or mounting the stairs. But there she was, looking in the mirror over the bathroom basin, seeing her face all blubbered with tears, seeing her own sick pallor, the dark horror of her eyes. She shuddered and covered her face with her hands. What a mess she had made of things !

But still, having made the muddle, she must clear it up. Her whole shattered little world gathered itself together and began to spin on this new axis. She was a fool and a coward, she had fallen weakly under Terry's spell like any ageing, sex-starved spinster ; she had been blind, and she had been silly. But she could be different. It was another moment like the one she had known when she had realised her dependence on Elsie. That moment had resulted in a metamorphosis and this was the same ; it generated movement and decision.

She took a bath, chose a becoming dress, made up her face, and brushed her curls with brilliantine ; she would not *look* pitiable, at least. Just before leaving her dressing-table she opened a drawer and took out Grandmother Shadow's Indian jewellery, part of the legacy she meant for Elsie. One of Grandmother Shadow's brothers had brought the stuff back with him from India, and his sister had treasured it and regarded it with respect, only wearing it on very grand occasions. There

was a necklet, two bracelets and a pair of ear-rings, all
made in native silver, so soft that it was malleable,
and the design was rather like a daisy chain, intricate
flowers, worked with patient, perfect detail so that even
the stamens were separate and discernible.   The centre
of each flower held a jewel, a pearl, a ruby, an emerald,
very small, not very valuable, a mere finishing touch.
Fastening the ornaments about her throat and wrists,
Penelope had a clear and vivid memory of Grandmother
Shadow, so stern, so upright, so powerful in her tiny
world, so much a stranger to anything like muddle and
compromise and cowardice.   How sadly and how scornfully would Grandmother Shadow have regarded the
position in which this, the last member of her family,
found herself !

Feeling as though she were about to face the ending
of the world, Penelope went down to the drawing-room,
and, forgetting her ancestress for a while, drank two
gin-and-bitters, not the single glass of sherry which
would have been the utmost limit of Grandmother's
indulgence.   She heard Terry's motor-cycle roar in the
drive, and a moment later Terry ran past the door, calling, " I won't be a minute," just as usual. And as usual
he was twenty ; then, cleaned and brushed, he dashed
downstairs again and they went into the dining-room.

Everything was quite tasteless and difficult to swallow
and the meal seemed interminable.   There was a time
when Terry would have sensed something wrong, probed
her mood, and managed in his own inimitable way to
lighten it.   But now he had troubles of his own, and
beyond saying, " You look very grand, is anyone
coming ? ", he ate in silence broken only by the minimum
conversation of politeness.   When the meal ended
Penelope said, " Terry, I want to talk to you."   He
looked confused and guilty, for the matter of the cheques

was on his conscience, and he followed her into the
drawing-room with a sheepish expression and a mind
that was rapidly marshalling excuses.

As soon as the door was closed Penelope said bluntly,
"Terry, you remember back in the spring, I told you
that if ever you wanted a divorce you'd only to ask?
The time has come now, hasn't it?"

Despite the misery of the last few hours, despite her
strong feelings on the subject, she was speaking diffidently,
gently. The habits of a lifetime were not easily discarded. But to Terry it seemed as though a bomb had
exploded within a few feet of him. Even his practised
duplicity could not keep the colour steady in his face, or
his voice normal. Dirty white beneath his summer's
tan, he said, shakily defiant, "I don't know what you're
talking about." Great God, he thought, did ever a man
have such foul luck? They'd been so careful; taken
such elaborate precautions not to be seen together;
taken such elaborate precautions in another direction,
too. And failed on both scores. Now, on one side he
had June, certain that she was pregnant and vixenishly
savage about it, on the other Penelope who had obviously
heard something. And all the while he had been wasting
thought and effort over the business of those cheques.
He wasn't prepared for this. "I don't know what you're
talking about," he said, bidding for time.

"Oh, Terry! Don't make it worse. That girl—
Miss Axten—she's back in the village, and she's pregnant.
Everybody is talking about you and her. I can't bear it.
I really can't bear it, Terry. I want to divorce you and
clear up the muddle. You'll have to marry her, now."

He said, still thinking rapidly, "Sit down, Pen.
You're shaking like a leaf. My dear, who said these foul
things to you? It isn't true. I parted from her in
February. Didn't I give you my word? If she's back,

well, her home is in the village, I can't stop her coming
here. And if she's pregnant—well, Pen, I told you
what she was. She's probably had a dozen men since
then. It isn't my doing. I swear it isn't." He flung
out his arms, not acting any longer, genuinely fired with
self-pity and fury. "My God, was ever a man so
punished for one lapse? To hear you say . . . to know
that you've been thinking . . . Darling, what can I
say? What can I do to prove that it isn't true?"

That part of Penelope which shaped stories and took
charge of dramatic situations laid a cool hand on the
arm of the Penelope who was just a woman hearing
words which she wanted to believe.

"You could bring the girl here," she said. "I think
I should know if she were telling the truth."

"Of course you would," he cried—and there was a
genuine note in his voice again. For surely Pen did
have the devilish way of seeing through everybody
except himself. And he would threaten June, if it
came to that he'd tell her that if she betrayed him
he'd never, never marry her, no matter what Pen might
do. "I'll fetch her right away," he said.

Oh God, thought Penelope, now more than half-
convinced. Her mind, so adept at foreseeing situations,
began to see this one; and her heart, so ready to put
itself in another's place, began to shudder with pity
for the girl. If what Terry said was true—and his
willingness to put the matter to the test was almost
proof enough—then how would the girl feel, being
dragged here and asked questions that no one had a
right to ask. And the whole thing was so likely. The
girl was lovely; she was loose, or she wouldn't have
been caught like that at the farm. What more likely
than that she should get into trouble? What more
likely than that she should, in trouble, return to the

only home she knew? And what more devilishly
certain than that her condition should, by village gossip,
be attributed to Terry?

And having reasoned so far, she abandoned reason
and gave way to emotion. It wasn't true. Terry
belonged to her, as, he had assured her, he had always
done in his heart. She hadn't to face a divorce, to
have everybody saying, well, what did she expect?
She hadn't to face living alone.

"Well," said Terry, who had watched, breath suspended, the changes racing over Penelope's face. "Shall
I fetch her, or do you believe me? "

The thought that she had wronged him ; that she
had believed, even for an hour, the things beastly people
were saying about him, made her cry, "Oh Terry,
I'm so sorry, please forgive me," a cry from the heart.
And Terry's relief from strain took the form of emotional
extravagance upon his part, too. The process of "making
up" was violent in its tenderness. But after the full
tide had flooded and begun to recede, each mind bore
a scrap of flotsam on its washed surface. The one on
Penelope's mind was the thought that never again
could she be comfortable in the presence of Agnes and
Florrie. And while she was thinking about how, and
when, and why to dismiss them, Terry was remembering
that the dangerous moment had been merely postponed,
not averted. June was set upon marriage now ; and
if only he could lay hands on some real money he would
not trouble how soon Penelope knew. On the other
hand, if it came to a choice between keeping one woman,
and being kept by another no one but a fool would
hesitate. What to do, where to turn ? He was not—
and Penelope had never succeeded in making him—a
consumer of books, and, apart from the sporting pages,
he hardly looked at a paper. That was a pity, for in

their different ways both books and newsprint could have informed him that the position in which he found himself had baffled cleverer minds than his. Yet he reached, during a hot August and sultry September, the same conclusion as had come to other men. And he laid certain plans. The trouble was that he was, as far as his cold nature permitted him to be, very fond of June Axten. So fond that life without her held few charms. So he hedged, and persuaded, and argued and threatened ; and waited and schemed.

Agnes and Florrie had gone and their place had been taken by another " decayed gentlewoman," a Mrs. Stornaway. Penelope had engaged her deliberately, though not without misgivings. Still, she had thought, whatever this woman's poses, phobias and pretentions, she would, at least, not gossip in the village. And Mrs Stornaway, who was very unprepossessing in appearance, and almost stone deaf, settled into the Dower House as into a haven. She liked housework, liked the country, was mildly fond of Penelope and mildly tolerant of Terry Domestically, the Dower House had a peaceful late summer and autumn. Penelope, happy again in her Fool's Paradise, thought less and less often of June Axten ; and never guessed that Terry was once again engaged in stripping the Yew Tree Farm of everything saleable, so that amongst the menfolk of Canbury his curious agricultural methods were as great a source of interest and gossip as his putative fatherhood was amongst the women. June herself was seldom seen, and Terry's interviews with her were now as few as he could make them. For they all followed the same pattern, tears, abuse, threats and tears again.

It was during a prematurely cold spell of weather in the middle of October that she put a threat into action.

Owing to her deafness Mrs. Stornaway was a poor
answerer of bells, so it was Penelope herself who, shortly
before mid-day on a Wednesday morning, went shivering
to the front door in answer to a peal. The wind was
on the front of the house and as soon as she had turned
the knob the pressure of it flung the heavy door against
her, so that she was obliged to cling to it, almost
wrestling for a moment, then, shaking back her hair
and blinking short-sightedly, she looked at the figure on
the top step and recognised June Axten. She was, if
anything, prettier than ever, with a scarlet chiffon scarf
tied fisher-girl fashion over her hair and under her chin,
and the growing bulkiness of her body concealed by
the folds of a swagger coat of cheap, but becoming fur.
Penelope knew, by the mere glance of recognition, why
she had come, and what she was going to say ; and for a
moment she was seized by an impulse to say, " Go away.
I know everything. There's nothing you can tell me."
But the girl was already saying, in a prim, constrained
voice, " Can I speak to you for a moment, Mrs. Munce?"
and natural good manners triumphed once more.

" Of course. Come in," said Penelope and tried to
close the door. The wind was too strong, and after a
second the girl stretched a long arm above Penelope's
head and lent her strength to the task.

" Thank you," said Penelope breathlessly " Now,
will you come this way ? " She led her into the warm
bright study which only a minute before had seemed
such a pleasant place.   And as she did so she remembered
the easy grace of the gesture, the strength of the out-
stretched arm, and thought, unwillingly, but she is
magnificent, too. Beautiful and strong and unmarred
by *this* ; what a pity that it all has to be so sordid !
And at the same time she felt her own stomach quake
with a sick nervousness.

"Do sit down. And loosen your coat. It's warm in here."

The girl obeyed her. The thrown-back coat left the great promising curve of her body revealed. She wore a scarlet and white smock over a plain black skirt and Penelope, looking at her covertly, knew a twinge of respect. She hadn't gone to pieces or lost interest in her appearance as so many people in her position would have done. She has guts, thought Penelope : and would have been surprised to know that her own position would have been very different if June Axten's vanity had been less strong. It was because June, despite everything, was still personable and attractive, that Terry, in all his schemes, had trimmed the balance in her favour.

Penelope saw the girl moisten her lips, saw her throat move. As much from pity as from impatience to have the thing done, she said,

"I think I know what you have come to tell me."

A certain relief showed on the beautiful face ; but June said, a little truculently, "If you know I'd have thought you'd have done something about it."

"Exactly what do you expect me to do ? "

"He always said you'd divorce him if it happened again. Now you can see it did. I guess he was afraid to tell you. So I had to. I can't go on like this no longer. I know it's a funny thing to come saying, and a funny thing to ask. But if Terry hadn't sworn you'd get rid of him next time I wouldn't have gone with him no more. I didn't bargain for this anyway."

"No, I suppose not. Well, what Terry said was quite right. I wouldn't stand in your way for the world. It's just that . . . well, Terry hasn't been frank with me about it. Now that I know . . . ."

The great dark eyes flashed. "Frank . . . I should

say not. He couldn't be frank to save his life. I know
that now. He's had me right and left, one way and
another. You ain't losing no treasure, Mrs. Munce, queer
as it may sound. He's no cop. But you gotta let him
go and I've gotta marry him. There it is in a nutshell."

"There's no legal compulsion on anybody," Penelope
said with gentle rebuke. "The decision to divorce
Terry rests with me, you know. And whether he . . ."

"But you promised . . . I mean he said you did.
You remember, back in February, you told him and he
told me . . . Look, he isn't much use to you any more.
If it ain't me it'll always be somebody. You ain't
suited. We are in a way. I can make him marry me
and I can make him toe the line afterwards. I know I
can. You wouldn't want to keep your hooks on somebody that was always hankering . . ."

"That will do," said Penelope. "I certainly did
promise Terry his freedom, just as you say. And he
shall have it. I ought . . . it ought to have happened
in February. It would have saved a great deal of
trouble . . . and pain." She resisted an impulse to
tell the girl about the conversation with Terry in the
summer. Terry had lied then. But the girl must deal
with that. She seemed confident in her ability to handle
him. Let it go.

"I'll talk to Terry this evening and set things in
motion at once."

"Thanks." June rose and hooked the fur coat at the
neck. 'I'm sorry, really I am. It's funny . . . I mean
. . . Well, you have been awfully decent about it all . . ."
The last words came out in a rush. "Don't bother. I
can manage the door," she said.

She left Penelope feeling very small and defeated.

Her mind tried to take refuge in trivialities. She
must tell Mrs. Stornaway not to bother about lunch.

She must tell Terry to take his things down to the farm,
he mustn't sleep here tonight She must get into touch
with Oliver Watling. She must tell Mrs. Stornaway
about lunch. She must . . . Well, Mrs. Stornaway
first.

There was some pastry, half-rolled out, on the kitchen
table ; but Mrs. Stornaway, wearing two cardigans, one
ginger-brown and one maroon, was seated in a chair by
the fire, her head in her hands.

" Is anything the matter ? " bellowed Penelope. It
was very difficult to make a question both audible and
sympathetic.

" I feel ill," said Mrs. Stornaway simply. " I didn't
feel well when I got up, but I hoped it would work off.
I feel cold and my limbs ache. I'm afraid it's influenza.
You'd better not come near me."

Infection was one of the things Penelope did not fear.
She had never " caught " anything in all her life. And
she was glad to have something to think about. The
novelty of waiting upon someone else, eased her mind.
She took Mrs. Stornaway's arm, helped her upstairs,
put her to bed with an extra blanket and two hot-water
bottles and then took her temperature.

" It's a . . . little up," she said, shaking down the
thermometer hastily and biting off her first incredulous
exclamation. One mustn't tell the patient that her
temperature was one hundred and four.

" I think I shall get Doctor Carter to look at you,
Mrs. Stornaway," Penelope said, placing herself where
the woman could see her face, and articulating carefully.

" All right, thank you," said Mrs. Stornaway ; and
she added, pathetically, " The insurance'll pay him."

Doctor Carter, brusque and busy, said that there was
an epidemic of influenza about ; he gave Penelope
instructions to do almost exactly what she had done

already and said that he would look in later on, probably mid-afternoon.

Penelope, left looking at the telephone, meditated calling Oliver Watling at once and asking him what to do—how did one set about getting a divorce? But something stayed her hand. Perhaps, she thought weakly, it would be easier to talk to him. Perhaps she would need to go to Strebworth for medicine and things after Doctor Carter's visit and she might manage to see Oliver for a moment then. Or it might be easier to write. One could make things clearer that way; and suffer less embarrassment. Nevertheless, she *would* start now to carry her plan into action. So she picked up the telephone again, and when Terry's voice answered, she said, with deliberate restraint, because one never knew with telephones, " Terry, you'd better come over and take what you need for the night and sleep at the farm. I think you'll know why." And then, into the babble of incoherent expostulation at the other end of the line she dropped a sentence, almost casually. " I had a visitor this morning. Yes. I'd rather not talk about it. You know . . . you knew how I feel about it. Just come and fetch your things."

Doctor Carter arrived at three o'clock. He took Mrs. Stornaway's temperature and found it exactly one hundred point four. If he had liked Penelope he would probably not have mentioned his suspicion, but as it was he derived some peculiar satisfaction from stating his belief that the temperature had never been higher than that, and that Penelope, mis-reading the thermometer, had panicked Penelope, already a little strained in temper, and at the same time aware that small things, held close to the eyes, were not, with her, matters for much certainty, met this accusation in the worst possible manner, first defending herself hotly

and then recanting, saying, "Well . . I might have made
a mistake, but does it matter?" so that Doctor Carter
was confirmed in the opinion he had formed of her
during her unfortunate convalescence—an irritable, un-
balanced, silly woman.

"She'll be all right," he said, on the landing outside
Mrs. Stornaway's room. "Keep her in bed, on slops.
No food until the temperature is normal—normal is
marked, you can't mistake that. And she shouldn't get
up until it's been normal for two days. I'll give you a
prescription for some powders that'll ease the pains she
complains of."

Penelope drove with the prescription into Strebworth,
got the powders, bought lemons and grapes and a big
bunch of hothouse chrysanthemums for Mrs. Stornaway's
room, and drove home. Terry had been and gone during
her absence. There was a note addressed to her propped
on the hall table. The sight of the careful, schoolboy
writing sent a pang to her heart. But she felt her mood
harden as she read the words he had written.

"Looks like you *want* to get rid of me. All right,
go ahead. But she's got no proof and I shan't marry
her. Darling, I couldn't live with anybody after having
you." Just his typical muddled reaction. There was
another sentence, heavily scored through, at the bottom
of the page. What had he written and then regretted?
Holding it at arm's length and screwing her eyes Penelope
brought guesswork and imagination to bear. "Don't
worry about the milk," she read, "I'll put it outside
in the morning."

Queer, that that one bit of impulsive thoughtfulness,
scribbled over, should come so near to breaking her heart.

Darkness fell early; and the lower floor became
untenable. Desperately careful in checking items Penelope carried upstairs everything that Mrs. Stornaway

could possibly require before morning and a great many
other things beside.   At ten she gave her a final drink,
made her bed comfortable and left her.   At twelve she
looked in and found her sleeping peacefully.   Then she
spent two hours composing a letter to Oliver Watling,
and as Canbury clock struck two, crept into bed sur-
rounded by a loneliness and a silence that were positive,
menacing things.   She slept badly and dreamed wildly ;
but when she woke the window was bright, the morning
well advanced and she felt more refreshed than she had
expected.   Mrs. Stornaway, meek and grateful, reported
a good night and Penelope went down to the kitchen.
The milk stood on the step of the back door.   So Terry
had brought it, after all.   Beside it stood the carton of
cream, which, since her illness in the spring, Penelope
was in the habit of taking with her cereal breakfast ; one
of her spasmodic attempts to " build herself up."   She
carried it and the milk into the kitchen and then, having
made the pot of tea which Mrs. Stornaway had selected
from an assorted offering of " slops," came down and
prepared her own breakfast.   She was not conscious of
feeling hungry, but except for cups of tea she had taken
nothing since breakfast on the previous day ; also, to
eat properly when alone was a test of morale, besides
being sound good sense when one was nursing a case of
influenza.

It was, however, an unsuccessful precaution.   Soon
after breakfast she was feeling very ill herself.   She,
like Mrs. Stornaway, began to feel cold, conscious of
pains in her limbs and an aching head.   But she felt
sick, too, and there was a paralysing cramp in her stomach.
There was a form of influenza termed " gastric," wasn't
there ?   Nastier than the other.   And wasn't it the
devil that she should get it now, just when she was alone
in the house save for Mrs. Stornaway who was herself ill.

She sat crouched in a chair to ease the pain in her stomach until all her symptoms had merged into a vast feeling of illness. She felt ill all over; so ill that she could die. The thought went through her mind, and instantly a kind of half-puckish, half-puritan courage followed it. Imagine thinking of dying because one had the influenza! What nonsense. Of course she would feel worse if she sat here pitying herself. She recalled stories of the bad epidemic years ago, how mothers had nursed whole families and never betrayed the fact that they were ill themselves. She remembered Grandmother Shadow, going about her ordinary duties almost to the last—and riddled with cancer. Resolutely she rose to her feet and with the sweat breaking out on her forehead, climbed the stairs. She was just in time to be sick in the bathroom. Afterwards, glad that she had been able to reach the right place, and a little relieved by the sickness, she went in to see Mrs. Stornaway.

" Oh," said that lady, rising upon one elbow, " you do look ill. You've got it, I can see. You must go to bed at once. Never mind about me. I'm over the worst. You go and get into bed. Oh dear, that it should happen like this! But you go and lie down. You look as though you'd drop."

All Penelope's brave resolutions vanished before a fresh wave of nausea. Turning, she groped her way back to the bathroom and was sick again. Clinging to the edge of the bowl she brought the small remaining portion of her mind into play. She must get a nurse and the most likely person to help her to get one was Doctor Carter. Oh, why hadn't she had a telephone installed by her bed! The stairs again.

Doctor Carter's epidemic of influenza had been complicated by the beginnings of the Prendergast baby's arrival and by young Bobby Howes' appendix suddenly becoming acute. The poor man had been up until twelve, up again at four and was eating a belated breakfast just as Penelope's call reached him. And, as usual, Penelope struck a wrong note.

" Can you please find us a nurse? I feel dreadfully ill myself and I can't take care of Mrs. Stornaway."

No, he thought, with irritable injustice, you wouldn't be able to. You silly, spoilt little women are all alike —give you anything to do for anybody else and you go sick from sheer suggestion.

" What's wrong with you ? " he asked unkindly.

" Influenza, I'm afraid. I've been awfully sick."

" Well, I'll see what I can do. Nurses, are at a premium just now. You'd better go to bed, anyway. Isn't there anyone in the village . . . a neighbour ? "

" I couldn't reach them." She thought of the New House, closed since Arthur's death ; of Mrs. Paine, inaccessible by telephone.

" Is your husband there ? " Doctor Carter had formed an excellent opinion of Terry, both as husband and nurse, during Penelope's pneumonia.

" He's away——" said Penelope. Then she was sick again, and Doctor Carter thought she had broken off in tears.

" I'll come over. I'll do what I can," he said. There was no comfort in the promise and he hung up without waiting to hear Penelope's voice again. He was due at the hospital for this appendectomy ; and must look in on Mrs. Prendergast first.

However, just before twelve o'clock that morning, he rushed out to Canbury, and found, by the irony of fate, exactly the situation he expected. Mrs. Stornaway, in her shabby camel-hair dressing-gown, was out of bed, in Penelope's room, mixing a drink of lemon juice and water, and Penelope, half-undressed, was lying on her

bed crying. She was crying partly because she felt so
deadly ill and partly because, despite her shouted protests,
her housekeeper had insisted on leaving her bed and
making some attempts to play the nurse. But Doctor
Carter, who was the victim of personal and social prejudices, did not know that. He saw what he wanted to
see—Mrs. Stornaway, whom he had known for some time,
a poor honest woman whom he respected, being exploited
by her employer, a silly, hysterical, self-indulgent woman,
who—and here lay the whole crux of the matter, though
Doctor Carter had forgotten it with his conscious mind
—who had hair very much like that of a pretty girl who
had once, long ago, tactlessly snubbed a sensitive,
awkward young medical student.

He said fiercely to Mrs. Stornaway, " Didn't I tell
you to stay in bed ? " But he didn't shout loud enough,
and he wasn't looking her full in the face, so she stood
looking puzzled for a moment and then said, " Mrs.
Munce is very poorly " She looked ill herself, pale and
tremulous, and pathetic with her two thin plaits of
grizzled hair He almost pushed her away from the
bed and into a chair Then, grim and brisk, he took
Penelope's temperature, which was sub-normal, and
Mrs. Stornaway's which was higher than yesterday's,
and turned back to Penelope.

" Where is your husband ? "

" At the farm. But he . . . but I . . ." Oh, but
she was too ill to explain. Too ill to care.

" Well, he must come back and look after you. Probably he can get someone from the village. There isn't a
nurse or a woman to be got today, I'm sorry. But one
thing I can do. It's a risk, but the best thing I can
suggest. I'll take Mrs. Stornaway back and put her
to bed in the Cottage Hospital." He did not add,
otherwise she'll be up again as soon as my back is turned.

But he thought it. And so deaf is prejudice that he mistook reason for the relief in Penelope's voice as she gasped, " Oh, thank you."

He jerked out a few directions ; then, whirling round to Mrs. Stornaway, wilting in the chair, shouted his plan at her. There was kindness of a sort in him ; he fetched blankets and rugs and tucked them around her and carried her downstairs and packed her into the back of his car, piling wrappings about her. And he drove very carefully, especially along the bit of private road to the farm, where he told Terry to drop everything and go and look after his wife.

A mad situation. To die in your bed of gastric influenza—yes, and of shock, a shock you had been awaiting for months, and a broken heart, a heart that had broken gradually ; and to be tended by the man to whom you said take your things and go. A mad end. No, that wasn't it. They, the elders and betters, always threatened you with a bad end. You'll come to a bad end. They were right, too. It was bad. There was pain, and dreadful humiliation, and a kind of blankness as though everything had receded and stood off, watching, waiting. Terry was like that, too. Watchful, waiting.

She had tried, once. Yes, when he first came in. She had apologised, attempted a ghost of a smile ; and then, later on, in a fresh spasm of sickness, she had gasped out, " I don't think we'll need to talk about divorce, Terry. I think I'm going to die." But there was no response from Terry. She had offended him irrevocably. He might stand within arm's length at the side of the bed ; he might go through all the motions of attentiveness and care ; but he had gone. He had left her. She could see that by his eyes. They were cold and hard, calculating. The eyes of a stranger, dragged in against his will, to do certain things for a woman who meant nothing to him. There was shame in that.

She saved some strength for thought and planning, refusing to be swept away on this tide of dire ill-feeling. She said, "Terry . . . Miss Shrewsbury could find a nurse. A nurse from London . . . or somewhere."

He nodded, but the hard stubborn dislike on his face remained. It made him look cruel. And yet . . . yet, he had lighted the fire in her room ; he had undressed her ; her bed was tidy and now and again he moved the pillows. But his eyes were like stone, and watchful ; and his mouth was cruel.

Then it was night after the short twilight of the October day ; and the wind, high all day, rose to a fiendish height, screaming in the chimney and at the window, slashing the cold rain on the pains. Now was the time, when ordinarily a certain amount of illness was bearable, when the bed was cosy and warm, the room softly lit, the body relaxed in idleness and the heart soft with gratitude for the day's attention. But tonight was different ; the outraged body refused to give up its grudge and the gratitude was salted with shame and regret. Oh, how better far to be Mrs. Stornaway, impersonally attended.

Terry brought a glass of lemon juice and water. She sipped it and checked the weak complaint on her lips. He had used too much of the peel, there was a bitterness, a threat of sickness in the glass. She said, "Not now. Later perhaps," and he put the glass on the table by her side. He put a bell beside it and said, "I shall be next door. Ring or call if you want me. I shall hear."

She said, "Good night, Terry . . ." and then, with sudden tears of weakness and self-pity springing from her eyes, began her apologies again. He cut her short.

He said, " Oh, it's all right. Good night." Impatient.
Still angry with her.

And now, save for the wind, there was silence upon the
house. She lay very still against the pillows, cosy under
the soft light bedclothes, a hot bottle on either side.
Her mind cleared a little. She could think again. And,
with her faculty for putting herself in other people's
places, she began to think about the day's happenings
from Terry's point of view. Naturally he was angry
and uncertain. What else could he be? Last night
he had been banished to the farm. Tonight he was
installed as sick nurse. And she had never mentioned
his note. Yesterday afternoon it had seemed muddled
and heartless, all in a piece with his behaviour. But
perhaps he had meant it sincerely. Perhaps after all,
despite everything he was genuine in his protest that he
did not want to marry the Axten girl. Perhaps there
was a case to be made out for him. There was more to
love than sex, more to sex than love. They should not
be confused. June Axten would be good to sleep with—
anyone could see that ; but she, Penelope, might be
better to live with. Oh, God, moaned Penelope, seeking
a cool spot on her pillow, once you began to think this
way there was no end to tolerance. Life could have no
shape at all.

A small reasonable voice in her mind said, other men
have to make that choice, why should Terry be exempt?
Why should he have everything? But she ignored it,
asking herself again what she could do. Could she—
perhaps in another place, not Canbury—keep June
Axten and her baby and share Terry with them? But
that was polygamy. Well, what was wrong about that?
It wasn't bad in itself ; it was a question of custom and
tradition. Great civilisations had encouraged polygamy

—what about the Old Testament ? Perhaps that was what Terry wanted. Obviously he wasn't satisfied with Penelope as his wife ; yet he didn't want a divorce ; and he didn't want to marry June—if his note could be believed. On the other hand there were the girl's feelings to be considered. Would she be insulted ? Or secretly relieved ? Second fiddle . . . but favourite fiddle in so many ways. And she had said of Terry, " he's no cop "—and she would be financially secure.

Well, there was no point in tearing the mind to pieces now. If she lived—and she felt less like dying than at any moment since breakfast time, she would talk this all out with Terry. And one thing she would not do. She would not again rush into decisions because she was angry and ashamed. She would never think again about gossip and self-respect or sordidness. Perhaps this sudden illness had been just in time to save her from getting rid of Terry and then regretting it for ever.

A kind of peace, of lassitude rather than of relaxation, stole over her. She fell asleep and yet, in some curious fashion, knew that she was sleeping. She could see herself, small in the big bed, see her closed eyes and gentle breathing. She knew relief and pleasure. I am asleep, a healthy sign, I shall live and manage to put things right. Then the nightmare started. She saw herself grow smaller and smaller, until she was no more than a doll in size ; and the door opened and Terry came into the room, as much larger than life as she was smaller. His face was hard with hatred and there was an indefinable air of menace about him. He began, with cross impatient gestures to strip the bed. She clung with tiny hands to the edge of the sheet and cried with a thread of a voice that she was in the bed, not to be overlooked. But he went on, and in a second's time, lifted the sheet,

tossing it to the floor. Her hands loosened and with a
shrill despairing cry, no louder than a gnat's, she sailed
in a wide parabola through the air and knew that dreadful,
nightmare feeling of falling down through immeasurable
space.

She woke, gasping. The sweat stood on her forehead
and her hands were slippery with it. She was avidly
thirsty and turned to the glass of lemon water which
Terry had left on the table. In a moment, when her
heart had stopped racing and her toes crisping with
terror, she would reach for it and drink.

It was too bitter, but it was cool and wet. With
another's hand to hold it, or with a supporting arm to
lean upon while she drank, she would have drained the
glass. But to lean upon one elbow was exhausting,
and her hand was still shaking from the feeling of
falling, so that she spilt some liquid on the sheet. She
set the glass back carefully after sipping twice and lay
back.

She must have been asleep for some time before the
dream woke her ; for the fire was now a mere handful
of pink ashes under a heavy veil of grey and the bottles
were lukewarm. Only the little lamp had kept an
unchanging, steady vigil. The wind was still dashing
the rain at the windows, still howling like a demented
thing about the house.

And she felt ill again, with a cramp in the stomach, a
prickly tingle in hands and feet, a sense of deathly illness
all over. Going to be sick again. Going to ring the
bell. Having no time. Saying "Terry" in a silly
weak voice without carrying power. Too late. Being
sick. Nothing much ; just the lemon water. It *bounced*,
she thought with grim humour.

She lay back, thinking that there were still some hours
till morning. There was no point in calling Terry.

There was nothing he could do for her and his company, just now, held no comfort. She felt too ill to sleep ; and if she lay thinking about her woes she would feel worse. And she didn't want to go through the business of Terry-June-Penelope again. She had settled that and must talk to Terry. Think of something else. Come on. What was the good of being known in twelve countries for your inventive brain if you couldn't entertain yourself for a few hours. Make up something. Tell yourself a story.

No, don't bother to invent people, that takes too much effort and vitality. Just take people you know and weave a romantic, entirely incredible story around them. June and Terry will do.

Suppose now that there is a young man, married to an older woman, and he falls in love with a beautiful young girl. The older woman—oh, yes, call her Pen if you like, is willing to divorce him ; but that doesn't seem to be exactly what he wants. Why not ? Oh, because of the money, of course. He hasn't any of his own. And the young woman is, obviously, fond of pretty things, a rather expensive young woman in her way. What does the young man do ? God, no, I don't mean what did he do or what will he do . . . this is a wild, incredible tale, calculated merely to divert the mind. What *might* he do ? Imagine it very softly, make it a whisper of invention, but he might try to do away with his wife. That's the style, make it truly diverting. Sublimate that dream, use it. Entertain yourself by the menace that there was in that experience. Yes, the young man Terry, if you like, wants to kill his wife. Because she once told him that she had left him everything. You did tell him that, didn't you ? When you were ill and in a morbid mood. Yes, Pen had told Terry that ; so obviously he must strike quickly, before she began on the business of the divorce ; before even she could alter her will.

Now, how does he do it ? Well, poison is the safest method. Nobody knows, for certain, how many people die of poison each year. But several poisoners, when they are caught at last, confess to previous similar crimes —-so it argues that poison isn't as risky as, say, strangling or stabbing. Poison then.

And how administered ? Oh easy. She'd sent him off, you see, but she still had milk from the farm. On the step each morning, milk in a can, cream in a carton. And the cream was meant for her, specially. To make her fat. That is funny. To make fat the churchyard as they used to say of a green Christmas.

So she was poisoned, and died, and they put " Gastric influenza " on the death certificate ; because this invented Terry certainly did have the Devil's own luck, and there was an epidemic at the time, and the doctor had a notion that Pen always made a lot of fuss about a little illness. And unless he were a man honest and unself-seeking above the average run of men he couldn't, after that rather casual visit, suddenly voice suspicions even if he had them.

Well, she thought, there's your story, very neatly contrived. An overheated imagination may be a curse in some ways, but it has entertainment value. The habit of invention died hard.

And yet, what, after all, had she invented ? With another leap of the heart, another outbreak of sweat on her forehead and in her palms, she was bound to admit, nothing ! There was nothing unreal about that story except the hypothesis. If Terry had wanted her, not divorced, but dead, that was exactly what he would have done. It took only the elasticity of the writer's mind to encompass the possibility. Accept that and everything else fell into place. Everything. Even that scribbled-out sentence at the bottom of his note.   He had written it because his plan was already made and the milk loomed large in his mind ; and he had scored it out because he felt guilty about it. And in this light too it was clear why he hadn't said outright to Doctor Carter—I can't nurse her, she's turned me out. No, he must be in the house, so that if the first attempt failed he could make another.

But of course this was all rubbish. One was never murdered oneself ; no one one ever knew was murdered. People were. One read about them. But they weren't ordinary, humdrum, respectable people. In fact murder was so rare, so strictly area-ised, that if she, Penelope Shadow, lived to see Doctor Carter again and said to him, my husband tried to poison me, he would instantly say that she was suffering from delusions ; he might even have her shut up.   That was a sign of madness, wasn't it. Persecution complex carried very far.

No, suppose it were true, and she knew it, not as an imagined possibility but as an actual fact, she could never tell anyone. They'd remember that she forgot things and changed her mind, and was almost a recluse, and lived by the making-up of tales. They'd say she was mad, that she had always been a little—well, you know—*queer*. No, no one would believe her.

Not that they needed to. Because of course it wasn't true. It was the speculation of a mind running out of gear. It was the sick effort of a sick mind to entertain itself. Good God, Terry was a little unreliable about money ; he was unfaithful ; he was a liar ; but a murderer, no. A thousand times no. Really, when you came to think about it, it was very wrong even to imagine such things.

She turned her head and the glass of lemon water came within her eyes' focus. Obeying a sudden impulse she reached for it and emptied it on to the carpet in the space on the far side of the bed. Then she stood it back and lay down again, with her eyes fixed upon the window, watching for the first sign of dawn.

With the first faint greyness she could hear Terry awake and astir. Presently he came in and snapped on the centre light. She saw him glance at the empty glass, and something that she had not known before, sheer black terror, struck through her. Only for a moment. There was something so ordinary about his perfunctory, half-sullen inquiry as to how she was feeling that denied the fantastic suspicion in her mind. Surely he'd pretend more. All the stories told of smiling, silken-mannered poisoners. This was just a sulky boy who felt—with some justice—that he was being messed about, imposed upon, made use of.

" I was sick again. Only a little. I don't feel any worse," she said in answer to his question.

" I thought I'd get your fire going and then go to the farm for half an hour. Is that all right ? Would you like a drink or anything first ? "

" No, thank you. Nothing." Two pairs of eyes turned to that empty glass, and then away again. But it must be fantasy. It must !

He got the fire quickly. He had always a curious facility for lighting fires ; admirable and incomprehensible to Penelope who could use stacks of paper, bundles of dry wood and pints of paraffin oil and still have no fire at the end of an hour.

" When you come back I'd like some tea. Just tea, please."

" Right-o. I shan't be long." His manner and his voice were still unfriendly.

She heard the car start. The wind had dropped a little and there was no more rain. The window paled rapidly.

Half an hour. He would be back in half an hour.

She set herself a test. When he came again, with tea on a tray, could she drink it ? No, face it ; it must be faced. Could she drink tea, or anything else, made by Terry. Because if not, it proved that part of her mind did believe that self-made story ; and a situation, awkward to say the least of it, was going to arise. Because, thought Penelope, good and thick as that carpet is, there is a limit to what it will absorb. Not to mention the look of the thing, full cup, empty cup, full glass, empty glass. Besides, I can't starve. I'll want something sometime.

Suddenly something snapped in her mind, or in her soul, or in that imponderable known as character. It was too much, she thought, bursting into tears and making no attempt to check them. Granted that everything she had thought in the night was nonsense, even then, even then, she was ill, and all alone. The position between her and Terry was an impossible one. She was ill ; and mad as well. And I have tried, she cried inwardly, in an ecstasy of self-pity ; I have tried.

She made a rapid mental review of her life. Apart from being self-absorbed she hadn't done much harm. She'd been a bit blind over Elsie, but she'd tried to put that right. And she'd married Terry . . . but then he had asked her . . . or as good as. She'd worked hard, and not flung her success about in people's faces, and she'd never deliberately hurt anyone. A negative virtue, since to hurt other people would have hurt her, but still, she hadn't ; and it did seem hard that she should lie here, really ill, tended by grudging hands, and being racked by crazy thoughts. What have I done ? she demanded of the quiet house. And there was no answer, except the one she could give herself. I've just been myself, muddled and foolish.

Well, then, since that has got you nowhere, stop being yourself. Beat your way out. Escape.

From what ? Why, this intolerable situation.

But how ?

There she lay in the big bed ; her eyes hollowed and darkened as by a long illness ; her skin dry, her lips cracked and sore, a look of emaciation already visible, and the last illusion of youth gone now that her tendrilly hair was flat and limp. A poor little ageing creature, sick, doubting her own sanity, and broken in spirit. A pitiable little object to any observer, had there been one who could see and understand.

But the whole of Penelope Shadow did not lie there, broken and distracted and done for in the big bed. If we are part of all we have been, how much more are we part of all we have made ? And this woman, simple to absurdity, weak-nerved to the point of mania, this harmless, kind, shy little creature, had, in her day, made and known and understood some remarkable, courageous, fiery, indomitable men and women. In this very month of October people were reading the story she had started on the day when she first saw the predatory clutch upon Terry's arm ; they were thrilling to something unusual and stirring and oddly personal in that picture of Tudor England, just as they had thrilled to the same qualities in earlier work from the same hand. And now, in this low and critical moment, something in Penelope, something which had understood courage and resource and action, though she herself

had never been brave or resourceful or active, stirred
and shook itself. The pirate woman, Jane Moore, the
Aztec girl, Xhalama, the misunderstood Tudor states-
woman and others of their blood, stood by the bed,
urging her to save herself . . . and to justify them.

They took charge. It was the inventive mind which
asked, what is the first thing to do? And answered the
question with an uncompromising—To get away while
you can.

Moving with the uncertain, fumbling, tremulous movements of an imperfect robot, or a person in the extreme
decreptitude of age she left her bed. She put on a pair
of woolly slacks and a woolly coat, and over them a
housecoat of velvet, zipped all down the front. They
were easy to find, easy to put on, and adequate. Then,
going from piece to piece of the furniture for support,
she groped her way to the landing cupboard and found
her winter snow-boots, also zipped and fleecy-lined.
Her mind was clear enough, bent on its one objective,
though the top of her head seemed to hold a heavy
cannon-ball which moved and smote her sickening blows
with every step and tried to knock her senseless when
she stooped. Now she was dressed. Now for the
stairs. Clutching the banister, one step at a time, she
descended and was in the hall. Now what? Run away
and hide? But that was impossible. Even Jane
Moore, who had risen from childbed and gone to the
byre to milk cows; even Xhalama who had braved the
sacrificial altars of the priests; even Elizabeth Tudor
who had fought death, standing, for days—even they
agreed that to run was impossible.

But the inventive mind was undaunted. Terry would
come back in the car, and he would drive, as usual, to
the back door. He would enter the house, and probably
go straight upstairs. It might be just possible to hide

in the scullery whose door stood cheek by jowl with that of the kitchen, crawl out, say, when he was on the stairs, get into the car and start it. It would be warm, it would start easily, and to drive it would not demand an overwhelming physical effort. Her imagination gave her a reassuring picture of the car skimming along like a bird towards Strebworth and safety. After that . . . not so good ; but she would deal with that moment when it arrived. Even if they said she was mad—what did it matter ? She would go to the Hospital. They would hardly turn her away.

She reached the little scullery, saw that the door to the yard was unbolted, and the one to the kitchen closed, and then sank down on the floor. Crouched there, she was sick again. Influenza ? Poison ? Nervous excitement ? She could not know.

She heard the car purr round and stop ; heard the heavy slam of the door as Terry pushed it to behind him. Now he was in the kitchen, separated from her by the mere thickness of a wall, and half of that window. She could hear the pop as he lighted the Calor gas-ring, and the flow of water as he filled the kettle from the tap. Now there was the sound of a cup being set in a saucer, the little silver tinkle of the spoon. He was making the tea. Not running upstairs to inquire how she felt, not friendly any more ; merely dutiful, making the tea for which she had asked. Even now, even when she was on her way, waiting to fly from him and his possible schemes, from the wickedness she suspected, she could spare a flicker of emotion because things had changed so much.

But another emotion shouldered everything else aside. She knew that, if she could rise and peep through that window, she might, she *might* find the answer to her uncertainty. She dragged herself upwards, and clung to the edge of the small sink which stood immediately under the window. A little thrill of genuine excitement ran through her veins, carrying terror, and horror, yes, and a thread of pleasure with it. Her palate for the dramatic, always keen, savoured the moment. Now . . . now . . . ! But the instant after came the flat feeling of self-criticism ; ah, she knew that so well, too. Is it valid ? Is it credible ? Would anyone really act that way ? And at once, with a weakening of her hold on the sink's edge, and a lessening of her whole vitality, she knew that she was crazy. She had told herself a story and come to believe it. She *had* become a victim of persecution complex. Imagine any woman leaving her warm bed and skulking in a scullery to spy on her husband making a cup of tea ! Ridiculous. Grotesque absurdity.

He warmed the pot. He measured in the exact amount of tea. He poured on the boiling water. The little tea-pot lid, creamy-white with its dainty wreath of painted convolvulus lay there ready to hand. It had suddenly a pleading air—put me in place; please, that is good tea, it is ready to be covered, stop now and drop me into my place.

But Terry hesitated. The thin column of steam rose from the uncovered pot. He stared at it. Hesitated still. Hunched a shoulder, in a gesture that was indescribably eloquent and final and then reached for a pocket somewhere inside his jacket.

You're seeing this, Penelope Shadow, who all your life have indulged in vicarious living. You're in your own scullery, more or less in your right mind—your sight is good anyway, long sight and good. And you see him, see the handsome sullen face and the bright auburn hair, the dark-stubbled chin, unshaven as yet, the red polo-necked jersey, the tweed jacket. The jacket, with a pocket on its inner side. And you see him take a screw of paper, untwist it, shake something whose flow is too brief and too thin to be stated in terms of colour and substance, into the steaming pot. And then, too late, the innocent little flowered lid is lifted into place. Borgia and a tea-pot. Madeleine Smith and the evening cup of cocoa. Don't waste a thought on whimsy now, Penelope ; the time for little quips is past. You know now.

Did the breath go out of her body in an audible gasp ? Or did some involuntary movement of horror make a stir on the air, already tense with guilt ? Or did those wide, hollow, disillusioned eyes peering above the ledge of the inside window, exercise some magnetic power ? He paused, with his hands outspread on either side of the tray and glanced sharply round the kitchen. Then he was at the door, glancing left and right about the empty yard ; then from a thrust of his hand the scullery door swung back. And there was Penelope, crouched and small, still clinging to the sink, quite helpless in the grip of such terror as she had never even imagined.

He was mad now, dumb with fury. Seeing him bear down upon her, feeling, rather than reckoning the strength of his hands, the power of his whole mad furious body, she shrank smaller, lifting her own hands and making piteous little mewing noises. They were pleas really, and promises. She would give him anything, do anything, go away and never, never say what she knew, if only he would let her go. But she was too frightened to be coherent, he too angry, too distraught to listen. He flung her bodily out of the scullery, lifting and throwing as he might have lifted and thrown a thieving cat. Her hands and knees made painful contact with the gravel of the yard ; the shock of the fall dazed her for a moment.

She heard herself saying, idiotically—" Don't hurt me ;
don't hurt me." And at the same time she began to
hope, also idiotically, that the worst was over. Terry
had been furious, aghast and beyond control with fury
at being caught in the very act. He had thrown her
down—and by that rough violent action he would have
relieved his feelings. Now . . . in a moment . . . he
would see that violence would do no good. He would
pick her up and she would be able to talk. She would
say all those things again. She would repeat the pleas
and the promises.

Into this idiot's dream broke a sharp sound ; a grating
creak, a reluctant, slow, scraping noise. She recognised
it instantly. It was the sound of the well lid when it
was first opened after a period of disuse. And the
thought sliced through her brain like a knife—he's going
to throw me down the well !

Then, as though the peculiar horror of the thought had
indeed cut her off from the normal roots of time and
space and reason, she had an experience of eternity. It
was like the cinema when it goes into slow motion.
Everything was very silent, and so slow that movement
was almost imperceptible. The well head was hardly
three strides away, out in the middle of the little yard ;
and Terry was not wasting any time. Yet, in the few
seconds which it took for him to complete the lifting
of the unwilling lid, return to Penelope and lift her, she
seemed to live and think through an immeasurable space
of time. First she saw the well—those steep wet walls,
with ferns in the upper crevices and the still circle of
water at the bottom. She knew that to the horror of
drowning there was something added ; horrors of heights,
claustrophobia—oh, obscene way to die ! And then she
saw how clever it was. Oh, clever, clever, even in blind
anger ; perhaps he didn't even realise how clever. Queer,

neurotic Penelope Shadow getting ill and going mad and drowning herself ; feasible ; credible.

And then, in this inch of time which stretched out taut and long, like elastic, she knew that there was only one thing to do. It might be done, by a superlatively clever woman . . . but could she, Penelope Shadow do it ?

Time, at least, was with her.

First, she must struggle and fight and make those three strides a hard battle. Yes, here were his hands now, lifting and grasping her. And he was surprised to find her fierce and resistant. It was a pitiable struggle, of course, the mouse wriggling between the jaws of the lion ; but it served. It brought him breathless to the well head ; and made the next contrasting move simple.

Now, with her feet and legs pressed against the brick-work of the well, she must collapse. Flat and finished, as good as dead now. She dropped through his hands. He was unprepared for the sudden limpness of the body which, a second before, had been resisting so fiercely. And because the struggle had been so sharp he stood for a second, catching his breath, leaving her as she had dropped.

And now, as he stooped to lift her again, came *the* moment. (Moment ? It is less than a second's space. In less than a second one body, Penelope or Terry, will be hurtling down to horrible death. Penelope is little more than a heap of clothes tumbled by the low circle of bricks ; Terry is strong and upright, has caught his breath again, is determined and desperate. Was ever an outcome so certain ?) He stooped, his hands ready to seize and heave ; and then, before the grasp was fast and sure, the limp body suddenly came to life again. It moved. To Terry it was rapid, acrobatic movement, to Penelope, whose mind was outstripping time it seemed a slow deliberate business. With hands braced against the little wall, feet gritted into the gravel, she raised her body until her back arched like a cat's. Terry, stooping forward, unsuspecting, to lift her, was actually himself lifted, was shot forward. His hands grabbed unavailingly at the chain-encircled roller. Then he was gone.

*　　*　　*　　*

" Keep that rug round you," shouted Doctor Carter, forgetting that Mrs. Stornaway had already gently mentioned the fact that in a car she could hear quite well, the vibration helped. He was disappointed in his role as champion of the underdog and furious with his protegée. And as his car rattled through the village of Canbury he hoped, with a spitefulness which he knew was childish and unworthy, that the Dower House would be locked and closed up and Mrs. Stornaway forced to admit that she had been wrong.

It was Wednesday now, and ever since Saturday, when Mrs. Stornaway had begun to feel better, she had been fretting and worrying about Mrs. Munce. Doctor Carter had said, and he had shouted, and he had bellowed that he had left word with Mr. Munce that unless his wife seemed well on the way to recovery by Friday, he was to let him know. No word had come from Terry, so the Doctor naturally assumed that Penelope's attack was as slight and as psychological as he had judged it. But would the woman take that for an answer? Oh, no. By Monday she had changed her tune; if Mrs. Munce were so much better it was queer that she hadn't written, or just rung up the Hospital to inquire for Mrs. Stornaway.

" She's so kind and thoughtful," she said, to Doctor Carter's amazement. " And she'd know that I should wonder. I can't understand it at all."

On Tuesday Mrs. Stornaway had, by pretending to be

anxious for her clothes, persuaded someone at the Hospital to telephone to the Dower House asking if someone could bring, or post her an outfit. Neither in the afternoon nor evening of that day could an answer be obtained from the Dower House. Doctor Carter, looking in to pay Mrs. Stornaway a fleeting visit, gave his opinion. The Munces had shut the house and gone away for a change of air.

"But Mrs. Munce would have let me know. I'm positive of it. She is forgetful, in a way; but she wouldn't just do that. She'd know that I haven't any clothes."

On Wednesday, Mrs. Stornaway could bear it no longer. "I'm going home," she announced with the ultimate, unshakable decision of the very meek. "Either she's worse and you won't tell me; or else she's just ill enough to be in bed and he's off out somewhere. The telephone is downstairs," she added, as though that explained everything.

"But you can't go home without clothes," protested the nurse.

"I can hire a car," said Mrs. Stornaway.

"Well, at least you must wait till Doctor Carter has been round," said the nurse, happily shuffling off this responsibility. "Then we'll see."

And Doctor Carter, knowing bull-headedness when he saw it, gave way and said that he would drive Mrs. Stornaway back himself.

"Then I can bring you back here when we find the place shut up," he said.

The car stopped before the front door.

"Now control yourself and sit still till I open the door," he said, checking Mrs. Stornaway's anxious descent.

The door was locked. He had expected that, some-how. He could just imagine Penelope, slightly ill, without help, rushing off to some comfortable hotel. He looked up at the windows. Not blinded, but then people often thought it safer to leave a house looking occupied.

" All shut up," he reported, returning to the car.

" Try the back," said Mrs. Stornaway. " Round this way is best." She pointed to the little path between the lavender hedge and the side of the house. He strode away.

Mrs. Stornaway gave him three minutes, and then, with the sense of foreboding which had been mounting for days, soaring to a climax of anxiety, she got out of the car and with a sweeping train of rug and blanket training behind her slippered feet, hurried along the path after him.

Mr. Munce's car stood by the back door, just as usual. The back door was open. The kitchen was a bit of a muddle and a tray, all ready set for tea, stood on one end of the cluttered table. There was no fire, and the kitchen was cold as a tomb.

Mrs. Stornaway discarded the most incommoding of her wrappings and holding the others higher, she hurried upstairs.

Doctor Carter was leaning over the big bed. Peer-ing round the obstacle of his body Mrs. Stornaway could see the figure he was examining, something so wasted, so sunken, so deathly pale that at the sight of it she cried out, a low, harsh wail of sorrow and despair.

" She's dead ! "

" No ! " he snapped. He dropped Penelope's flaccid hand, and said, as he strode the space between the bedside and the door :

" Turn on that stove ; heat some water ; find some brandy."

He was back by the time that Mrs. Stornaway had switched on the electric stove and had filled and plugged in the kettle in the bathroom. She padded back into the bedroom, saw the hypodermic syringe in his hand, winced as the needle drove home, and then, a little surprised at not having thought of it sooner, began to put up a hasty prayer.

" Hot bottles," said Doctor Carter. " We've got to get her warm."

Padding to and fro, Mrs. Stornaway filled Penelope's bottle, retrieved from the bottom of the disordered bed, her own, and then the big aluminium one which was kept for airing mattresses. The stove glowed, the room grew warm, and presently, between anxiety, and exercise, and physical weakness, and hard prayer and fantastic speculation Mrs. Stornaway was burning with heat. The idea struck her—I'm warm enough for two. And with the thought she darted to the bed and clutched that wasted little body to her own, holding it close, rubbing its hands, even pressing her own flaming face to its pale, shrunken one.

So when at last Penelope's mind flickered into consciousness she found herself in a kind and loving clasp with a familiar face looking into her own.

" She's back," said Mrs. Stornaway. But Doctor Carter had already seen the return of consciousness, and was ready with a glass of brandy and water. Mrs. Stornaway put out a masterful hand and held it to Penelope's lips herself.

It was nearly dusk before Doctor Carter could tear himself away from this unique case of life-saving. By that time Penelope had superseded Mrs. Stornaway in

that portion of his heart reserved for the under-dog ;
and beneath his professional calm he was as avid as Mrs.
Stornaway in curiosity to know how such an appalling
state of affairs could have come about.

" I shall call in at the farm on my way back," he told
Mrs. Stornaway. " And I'll collect Nurse Jewel and
bring her back myself. Keep the room at this temperature and keep giving her water. And don't ask questions
even if she seems livelier."

" When you're at the farm," said Mrs. Stornaway,
" tell them to send some milk."

Miller, who had acted as a kind of foreman at the
Yew Tree Farm, had no light to throw on the mystery.
" He went from here back to his brekfus, same as always
on the Friday morning, sir, and thass all I can tell you.
He just went in the office and then come out and I arst
him how Mrs. Munce was feeling and he said none too
well. Then he took the milk and went off . . . No,
that never occurred to me to wonder about him. He
bin away for spells afore. I just carried on with the
work and left him to mind his own business." A belated
glint of interest showed in the man's eyes. He had
remembered hearing some gossip about Terry, which,
because it did not seem to concern the farm work—
his sole interest—he had taken little notice of at the
time.

" Dint he go back to his missus ? " he asked.

" Nobody knows," said Doctor Carter shortly.

" Maybe he met with a naxident, pretty furious driver
he were."

" The car is intact in the yard of the house."

" Ah, but he rid a motor-bike at times."

" Well . . . don't forget to send along that milk,"
said Doctor Carter, climbing into his car and pondering

the chances of Terry having met with an accident in some
lonely lane or short cut . . . still, six days . . .

Mrs. Stornaway, with a skirt slipped over the lower
half of her dressing-gown and a cardigan buttoned closely
over the upper portion, lay in wait for the messenger
who would bring milk from the farm.   There were other
things she needed from the village.   Nurses liked comfort and nobody could eat bread six days old.   So she
watched the yard from the window of the landing just
outside Penelope's door and as soon as the boy on the
bicycle appeared, she opened the window and shouted
to him to wait.

She asked him into the kitchen to give him his orders,
because after all she was only convalescent, and her
health was very important now.   But she went with
him to the back door.   Standing there, looking out over
the yard for a moment, she noticed that the well-lid was
raised.   Curious, she thought.   The well was never used
in cool weather.   She stepped into the yard and then
stopped, feeling cold and frightened.   Stupid, she thought.
And yet, in such mysterious circumstances, anything
might be possible.   Anything . . . why . . . Mr. Munce
might be anywhere . . . the well, the car, any outbuilding . . . for that matter any room of the house.
She hadn't been through it.

Ashamed of herself, yet giving in to her fears, she
hurried back into the house, closing the door behind her.
But when Doctor Carter returned almost her first words
to him were, " The well lid's up.   It isn't usually.   Do
you think we ought to look down ? "

Doctor Carter took the torch from his car and proceeded to look down.

" It was just as well, really," said Mrs. Stornaway
later.   " I mean, well . . . doctors are used to dead
bodies, aren't they ? "

" I'm rather dreading the moment when she really comes to and asks about him," said Nurse Jewel. " I've never found sick people easy to fob off whatever they may say. Were they very devoted ? "

" She was extremely fond of him," said Mrs. Stornaway. " And he could be very charming . . . It all seems such a mystery. Such a tragic mystery."

The two women were enjoying a final cup of tea in Mrs. Stornaway's room. Across the passage Penelope, still looking like a corpse, but breathing normally, was sound asleep. Nurse Jewel wished heartily that Mrs. Stornaway were a little less deaf and a little less discreet. Still, gossip, even under difficulties, was enjoyable. So, hampered by their lack of knowledge, by the fact that the subtler inflexions of speculation were lost since whispering was impossible, and by the fact that every now and then Mrs. Stornaway said non-committal things, such as " he could be very charming," which might mean anything, the two pursued the inexhaustible subject. What had happened ? And how ? Had the dead man some secret worry, bad health, a love affair, financial trouble, severe enough to make him commit suicide ? Why had he gone to the well at all ? And having gone there was it possible that he had turned dizzy and fallen ? Had he, perhaps, been smitten by the prevalent influenza ? Or was it conceivable that he had been pushed ?

" But who was there to push him ? " demanded Mrs. Stornaway, as much of herself as of her companion. " Unless he had an enemy who was lurking about ? What's that ? I didn't catch what you said. Her ? Don't be silly ! Why, she was crazy about him. And she wouldn't hurt a fly. I am sure of that. Besides, she couldn't. I'd put her to bed with my own hands. She couldn't walk across the room after that last bout of sickness. I never saw anybody so ill. No, if there's one certain thing in the whole affair it is this. Mrs. Munce never left that bed from the moment I put her into it, to the moment when we found her there, practically dead. I'd swear that with my last breath."

She looked at Nurse Jewel quite fiercely. And Nurse Jewel, after a moment's thought, said, sagely, " Well, it certainly looks that way. I mean, if she'd done it . . . I mean if it was just *possible* that she'd done it, she'd have made some sort of arrangements to be found before she was so far gone herself. She was pretty near dead, you know."

" I know," said Mrs. Stornaway with the air of one who can be told nothing. " Doctor Carter said another hour would have been fatal."

They talked on ; saying all the things which Miss Penelope Shadow had arranged for them to say. She had written this conversation : written it as she turned into the empty house, crawled up the stairs and lain down to die, if need be, in order to end the tale convincingly. And this speculative conversation, begun by the nurse and the housekeeper, spread, before and after the inquest, over the whole neighbourhood. But it never varied its pattern. There were people who could, by stretching their imaginations, conceive that a small sick woman might push a strong healthy man into a well ; but they never mentioned the possibility because the next step was inconceivable. Nobody— because nobody else had a mind like Penelope's—could believe that a woman would deliberately lie down to starve, to thirst, to fall unconscious and miss death by an hour, in order to make an incredible story credible. No, it was either suicide or accident. And though there were those who knew that Terry had had reason for feeling suicidal, they held their tongues in public places. The jury's verdict of Accidental Death satisfied everyone.

Right up to the inquest, and through it, and for perhaps ten minutes afterwards, those good ruthless spirits, Jane Moore, Xhalama, and Elizabeth Tudor had stayed with Penelope. They had shown her how to escape, and given her the strength and cunning to escape unscathed. And then, quite suddenly, they deserted her. She was actually sitting at tea in the hotel where she and Mrs. Stornaway had taken up their temporary residence, and she was sipping a cup of pale milkless tea and thinking, well, it's over and done with. And then suddenly it *was* over and done with and Penelope was no more a clever, cunning, ruthless creature, but a gentle little woman with a conscience.

And that conscience was not troubled by thoughts of an act of violent self-defence, or by the memory of death coming suddenly to a soul quite unprepared. No, when Miss Shadow turned her back on the well and violated every instinct by entering that empty house, she had finished with Terry Munce. But now there was a fresh worry to nibble away at her mind. What about that beautiful girl and the baby soon to be born ? She was responsible for them, wasn't she ?

She brooded over her tea until Mrs. Stornaway became concerned. Mrs. Munce had been so brave, so sensible about the whole dreadful business, but it would be in keeping that she should break down now.

" You mustn't fret, you know," she said gently at last, interrupting Penelope's train of thought, busy with plans of charity—adoption—a laughing brown baby clinging to her hand and taking his first steps.

" I'm not worrying," she said, wrinkling her eyes in a smile. " I've remembered something I must do. I'm going to Canbury for an hour. And, Mrs. Stornaway, while I'm there, is there anything you'd like me to bring from the house ? "

Mad, thought Mrs. Stornaway, with regret and pity. Quite mad.

Still gently she said, " But you can't go there alone. Let me just change my shoes for something more comfortable and I'll come with you."

" There's no need, thank you," said Penelope ; and as she spoke a burden seemed to roll away. " I'll be all right by myself. I've got to see somebody first. And honestly I shan't mind going to the house a bit."

And it was true. The phobia had left her. She was now in every way qualified to be a lady living alone . . .

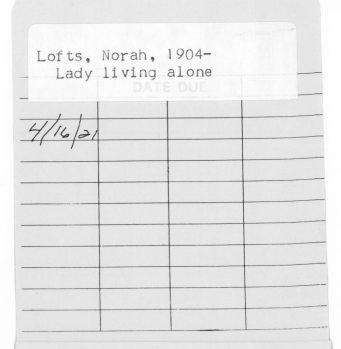

Lofts, Norah, 1904-
  Lady living alone

DATE DUE

4/16/21

PORTVILLE FREE LIBRARY

PORTVILLE, N. Y.

DISCARDED FROM THE
PORTVILLE FREE LIBRARY

Member Of
Chautauqua-Cattaraugus Library System